MYSTERY OF THE EGYPTIAN AMULET

Kid Detective Zet

SCOTT PETERS

BDB
FOR YOUNG READERS

Published by Best Day Books For Young Readers
Copyright © S. P. Wyshynski 2013
All rights reserved.

Mystery of the Egyptian Amulet/Scott Peters

ISBN 10: 0985985216
ISBN 13: 978-0985985219

**Visit Scott's blog, egyptabout.com, for Ancient Egypt homework resources,
free teacher worksheets, mummy facts, and so much more!**

CHAPTER 1
SNAGGLETOOTH

Twelve-year-old Zet stood outside a tall, narrow gate in the artisan quarter of Thebes. Time had blackened the metal with soot and age. It had taken human hands, however, to sharpen the tops of the bars into knife-like blades. Zet studied them a moment.

They'd be hard to climb over without getting ripped up pretty bad.

All around him, late afternoon shadows crouched low and dark. The dank smell of a leather tannery drifted from somewhere nearby, tugging at his stomach. It smelled like old urine. He tried breathing through his mouth. It didn't help.

"Hello!" he shouted through the gate.

No one answered.

He rattled the handle. Locked.

"Hello?" he shouted again.

It was hard to imagine his best friend Hui locked up in this creepy place. Locked up probably wasn't the right word, since Hui was there as a jeweler's apprentice. Still, it seemed like a jail, with its big, ugly unmarked entry.

Zet had been angry the whole way through town. You'd think Hui could've answered at least one of his letters in six months. Sure, Hui was probably busy. But that busy? Who forgets their best friend just because they land an important position at the Kemet Workshop?

He gave the bars a hard shake. It was still working hours. Where were these people? "Anyone home?"

A big man lumbered into view on the far side of the gate. His shoulders almost filled the narrow entrance as he approached. He was stripped to the waist, and sweat stood out on his barrel-shaped chest.

"Get away from here," he said.

Shocked, Zet frowned. "Isn't this the Kemet Workshop?"

"What's it to you?"

"I'm looking for a friend. He's an apprentice here."

"Apprentices don't get visitors. So beat it."

"But I just—"

"Beat it!" the hulk of a man said.

When Zet didn't move, the man cracked his meaty fingers. He took a key that hung from a loop on his leather belt and unlocked the gate. Zet stepped back a foot or two, but the man grabbed his arm and twisted Zet into a headlock.

"Makes a funny noise," the man said. "When your neck breaks. Crunch-like."

"I get it," Zet managed, seeing stars. "Let go."

The man spun him lose with a laugh, and Zet slammed face first into the dirt. Zet got to his feet, furious but trying not to show it. What would be the point? It was obvious the man would win any fight.

The man grinned, showing a set of jagged teeth. "We don't like snoops."

"I wasn't snooping. Just tell my friend Hui I was looking for him."

"Hui, huh?"

Immediately, Zet wished he hadn't said it. What if he got Hui in trouble?

Snaggletooth went inside and slammed the gate shut and locked it. "Hui," he repeated with a nod. "I'll tell him."

The thug walked away, knuckles cracking as he ground them into his fist. Zet swallowed and watched him go.

Something strange was going on behind that gate. Maybe there was a reason Hui hadn't answered. Zet wanted to climb over the knife-like bars, sneak past the guard and find him. But the workshop was probably a maze of rooms and corridors.

And who knew how many other Snaggletooth-like men lurked back there?

Running a hand over his short-cropped hair, he let out a frustrated breath. It took all his determination to turn his back on that gate, on Hui, and head for home.

CHAPTER 2
MISSING ORDERS

The next morning, Zet walked to work in a grim mood. The sun god spilled his rays over the rooftops as Zet wound through the narrow streets. He said nothing to his little sister, Kat, about last night's eerie visit to the Kemet workshop.

Still, she plodded along looking equally gloomy.

A woman stepped onto her front stoop, holding a broom. She shook it out. Dust rose in the still air.

"Good morning," she called.

"Morning," Kat said.

"Got to get things clean and ready for the Opet Festival," she said.

"Right!" Zet said, trying to sound cheerful. Her words, however, made sweat prickle on his neck. Sure he was worried about Hui, but he had another problem to deal with. And the problem kept growing worse.

He and Kat ran the family pottery stall—ever since their father had gone to fight the Hyksos invaders. Up until now, they'd managed pretty well. But things were going downhill fast. People had ordered a large number of special dishes and bowls for the festival parties, and the orders hadn't come.

Out of earshot, Kat spoke in a shaky voice. "Do you think the ship-ment arrived?"

"It better have."

"What if it hasn't? Our customers are really upset. They're saying things about us, like we can't keep up our end of the bargain."

"It'll come," he said.

"But it's been weeks. And like that woman said, the festival's almost here. People paid us in advance, Zet. They paid us a lot!"

He groaned. "Tell me something I don't know."

They reached the familiar marketplace. They were early, and none of the other vendors had arrived. The tented booths were still wrapped up, silent and deserted.

All, that is, except theirs.

Zet gulped. "Uh oh."

Half a dozen women waited. Frowning. Arms crossed.

Zet forced an uncomfortable smile.

His gaze flicked hopefully from the women to the surrounding area. He surveyed the whole marketplace, praying to see a crate had been delivered during the predawn hours.

But there was no crate.

"Maybe we should run away," Kat whispered.

He looked at her like she was crazy. "What, not open the stall? Come on, let's go."

Moments later, the complaints were flying.

"What was I thinking?" shouted a woman. "I never should have trusted a pair of silly little children."

"I planned three whole parties around the plates and platters I chose," said another in a trembling voice. "I've had table linens made to match, and centerpiece flowers and everything." She looked like she was going to start crying.

Anger Zet could handle, but tears were awful.

"They'll be here," he said. "I promise."

"For your sake, boy, I hope so," said the first. "Or I'll see you lose your stall for this."

With that, she and the others left.

To make matters worse, other vendors had arrived. They looked disgusted. They didn't want shady, unreliable businesses around.

Zet's stomach clenched. Lose the stall? But they'd starve. Sure, he'd earned a big reward several months ago, but he'd spent almost all of it repairing the damage to their business. And he'd promised his father that he'd take care of his sister, his mother and his baby brother.

His ears burned in shame. The thing is, everything the women said was true. They'd paid, and Zet hadn't delivered. The Opet Festival was just days away.

What could have happened to delay the orders?

On top of everything, he'd paid for them himself in advance to have them made.

Zet set out clay pots and colorful plates in the sunlight. The sun god's rays gleamed in the glazed dishes. He dragged a vase forward; taller than his waist, it scraped across the paving stones as he hauled it front and center.

His mind drifted from the stall's problems to Snaggletooth. Things might be bad here, but what was going on over at the Kemet workshop? Was his best friend, Hui, in trouble? Nothing about his visit the night before seemed normal. The more he thought about it, the stranger it seemed. Why would Snaggletooth put Zet in a headlock, just for asking to see his friend?

He glanced over at Kat. Her cheeks were still bright red. One woman had called her a crook, and a whole lot of other mean things. Kat stood alone, plate in hand, polishing it carefully. Even from here, he knew her well enough to see she was shaken. Sure, he and his sister fought like crazy, but she definitely wasn't a crook.

Kat really cared about making their customers happy. And so did he.

Noon came. The air felt stifling. Heat radiated up from the paving stones. The droves of shoppers slowed to a bare trickle.

"Kat," Zet called, wiping his brow.

His sister spun, black braids flying, a hopeful look in her dark eyes. Seeing his face, however, her look quickly faded.

"Oh!" she said. "I thought—well, I thought you saw the delivery people coming or something."

"No. I was just going to say we should go to the watersteps to eat."

She brightened. "And we can check for the pottery guild's shipping boat."

"Exactly."

"Wait . . . I don't know if we should." She crossed her arms and got that super practical look of hers. "It could get busy quick."

"We won't be gone that long," he said. "Come on, it will be nice and cool, and it would be good to relax."

She groaned. "I know. But you go. I'll stay. We can't afford to lose any sales."

"No. I'm in charge, and you're coming."

Which was true, seeing that he was a year older. Not that he ever made a big deal out of the fact.

"Thanks for the reminder, big brother," she said, rolling her eyes.

"Just come on," he said. "We need a break."

Kat glanced around the hot square. "Okay. But not for long."

Together they quickly tied a few linen sheets over their wares. From the stall next door, Geb, the herb-vendor, watched them over his baskets. His woven containers held herbs and spices for cooking, medicine and dyes—deep red powders, and mustard yellow, and Zet's favorite, bright blue woad—all piled high and shaped into cones.

When Zet and Kat picked up their lunch parcels and began to leave, the wizened old herb-seller shot them a surprised look.

Zet colored.

With their bad reputation growing, disappearing in the middle of the day was just making them look worse.

"We're not going far," Zet said.

"We're coming straight back!" Kat added.

Geb nodded. But the old man didn't smile.

CHAPTER 3
NO RECOGNITION

Kat twisted her braid as they exited down a shady lane that led
to the Nile. Neither of them said anything about Geb's disapproval, not to mention the rest of the market vendors. More
than one glare had come Zet's way.

Clearly wanting to change the subject, Kat said, "Don't you think
it's strange we still haven't heard from Hui?"

Zet shot her a look. All he said was, "Yeah."

"It's been six months. I'm sure they have scribes there. He could
have at least dictated a message. You know, like, 'hello, I'm having fun
making jewelry, and I have a million new friends, so I won't be writing
to you anymore', or something."

Zet was silent.

Somehow, he doubted friends had anything to do with Hui not
writing.

"I've sent him seven letters," she said.

Which didn't surprise Zet. She'd actually been glad when their father
hired a boring old writing tutor. And she'd actually paid attention. Then
again, boring or not, unlike most people, Kat could write, and fairly well.

"They were long letters, too," she said.

At this, he couldn't help a small grin. "They would be."

"What? What's that supposed to mean?"

Zet glanced at his little sister's red face. "*Someone has a crush,*" he sang.

"I do not!" Kat said, punching his arm.

"Ow." He laughed and leaped sideways. "Kat likes Hui!"

The bright patches on her cheeks deepened. "Quit it."

"Okay, okay."

Kat glared at him.

"Truce. Forget I said anything about Hui." He pointed ahead. "Look, there's the river. Come on, let's see if the boat's there."

A broad avenue ran along the river's edge. Here and there, wide steps led down to the water. People milled about. A musician sat plucking out a tune on a lute. Two men played a game of Senet, while a third watched.

The Nile sparkled, all full of bobbing birds and floating watercraft. Some boats ferried goods, and others carried passengers.

But the one boat they wanted to see wasn't there.

They stood in the shadow of a large Sphinx statue. Zet frowned at the spot where the potters usually tied up to unload their goods. He wished, by force of will alone, he could imagine the potters' boat into existence.

Suddenly, Kat gasped. "Look!"

At her tone, Zet's head snapped to where she was pointing.

A small boat held four people. In the back, poling them downriver, stood a huge, scary looking thug: Snaggletooth. In the front stood a second guard. A padded seating area filled the boat's midsection. In it lounged a man in a gold edged tunic. And beside the richly dressed man, sitting bolt upright, was none other than Hui.

Zet stared, unable to believe his eyes.

Hui looked different. Stiff and formal—completely unlike the joker Zet once knew.

The man in the expensive tunic said something to Hui.

Hui nodded, his expression blank and controlled.

On shore, Kat darted down the water-steps.

"Hui," she shouted. She cupped her hands around her mouth. "HUI!"

Everyone in the boat turned.

On land, Zet dove behind the stone Sphinx. From his hiding spot, he watched Hui's eyes fasten onto Kat's face. If he recognized her, he showed no sign of it.

"Hui," Kat shouted again, and waved wildly. "Hey!"

In the boat, Hui made no response. Instead, he simply turned away and stared straight ahead.

Clearly stunned, Kat let her arm drop. She watched the boat drift out of view. Then she turned to Zet.

"Did you see that?" she cried.

Zet nodded, mute.

"He didn't even know who I was. Did you see his face? He didn't recognize me."

"Maybe he couldn't see you clearly," Zet said, wishful.

"Of course he could. He looked right at me. Maybe he was hypnotized." She gulped. "Or possessed."

At this, Zet looked skyward. "Possessed? Come on." That was so like her, to think up something crazy.

"Well if he wasn't possessed or hypnotized, then—" She broke off. "Hey, wait, what were you hiding for?"

"Hiding?"

"Yes, hiding. When I turned around just then, you were all ducked down behind the Sphinx."

Zet rubbed his neck. It was gritty with dust and sweat. He wiped his palm on his kilt. "Well, here's the thing." He knew she'd be mad he'd kept it secret, but plunged ahead. "I went to try and visit Hui last night and it was all weird over there."

"Why didn't you tell me before?"

"Because we have other stuff to worry about. Look, I don't want to argue. Do you want to hear what happened or not?"

She snapped her mouth shut.

"They have this big black gate at the workshop, which is locked. And when I yelled to see if anyone was around, that thug in the boat came out and put me in a headlock for asking if I could visit Hui."

"He put you in a headlock?"

Zet showed her the bruises. "You weren't wondering where I got these?"

Kat's face had gone pale. "Not really. I mean, you're always getting bruises and stuff. Oh my gosh, Zet, that's totally creepy." She wound her fingers together. "Maybe he was hypnotized."

"I don't know . . . Maybe he's just busy with his new life. Maybe they don't like visitors over there."

Kat knit her brows together.

Zet hated to say it, but felt he had to. "Maybe Hui just doesn't want us around."

"That's ridiculous. Listen to what you're saying. Hui?"

Zet shrugged. "Maybe he's changed."

"Into a totally different person?" Kat demanded.

His eyes went to the boat, tiny now in the distance. It was true, that sure wasn't the Hui he knew—zany best friend and famous neighborhood trickster. Hui could throw his voice so it sounded like it came from a rooftop, or a doorway, or a window, among other crazy skills. That stiff Hui looked like he'd never stolen his mom's face paints and given himself fake bloody gashes and black eyes. He looked like he'd never jumped out and terrified Kat. But he had, a lot, and it had been totally hilarious.

Zet rubbed his face. "I don't know," he said. "Look, let's just go back to the stall. It's getting late."

She nodded, biting her lip. "I'm not hungry anymore, anyway."

"Hey," Zet said, trying to sound brighter than he felt. "You know what, I'm sure there's some explanation. Don't worry about it. Hui is Hui. He's probably got some scheme going on, and we'll find out about it eventually. Right?"

She let out a little laugh. "If Hui was just teasing me right then, pretending not to know me, I'll kill him."

From out of nowhere came a horrible thought:

If someone else doesn't kill him first.

CHAPTER 4
THE LETTER

S hadows closed over the city streets as evening fell. Alleys grew dark, doorways even darker. Overhead, red streaks stained the sky. Cool air brushed Zet's neck. He shivered, and walked a little quicker.

"Where are we going?" Kat asked, running to catch up.

"To talk to Hui's mom."

He rounded another corner and spotted Hui's house up ahead. It was two blocks from theirs. A lamp flared in the window. Even from outside, the chatter and shouts of Hui's little brothers—Akiki, Sefu and Moss—could be heard.

Zet and Kat mounted the steps and knocked on the wooden door.

"Coming!" called Hui's mom, Delilah.

She opened the door, looking cheerful as ever. Normally plump, now she was hugely pregnant. Her cheeks were flushed. Her hair, which she wore in ringlets, had a smudge of bread flour next to one ear. Her grin widened at the sight of them.

"Kat, Zet, hello."

"Hi," they said.

Instantly, Zet felt relieved. Obviously, everything was fine with Hui. His mom didn't look the least worried. Behind her, Akiki and Sefu ran past shouting. Over her shoulder, Zet spotted Moss climbing a ladder. Moss got his feet into the rungs, hung himself upside-down, and waved at Zet.

"Get down from there, Moss!" Delilah said, without even turning around.

Moss slipped and landed with a crunch and a wail. She went over, dusted Moss off, and set him on his feet.

"You'd better come in, and close the door," she said.

They did.

"I wanted to see if you heard from Hui," Zet said.

They followed her through the house, which somehow always had scrubbed floors despite the piles of wooden toys everywhere. In the kitchen, she gave a delicious smelling pot-full-of-something a stir.

"Got a letter yesterday," she said.

"You did?" Zet asked, baffled. If Hui had written to her, why not to him and Kat? Was his friend mad at them for some reason? It didn't make sense. "And he's okay?"

"Why wouldn't he be?" She pushed curls from her face and wrinkled her forehead.

Zet's fingers went unconsciously to his bruised neck, where Snaggletooth had grabbed it with his meaty hands. "I'm sure he is. That's not what I meant, I just wondered if he's happy. What did he say?"

"Actually, the letter wasn't from him." She paused. "Is something going on I should know about?"

Zet and Kat shot each other a quick glance.

"No," Zet said quickly. "It's just, we haven't heard from him, that's all."

"Well, if it makes you feel any better, neither have I. Not directly. It was a formal letter inviting me to what they call the six-month visit. It's very structured over there. But he's just busy, you know how things are, fitting in at a new place."

"There's a six-month visit? When are you going?" Zet asked.

"I'm not, unfortunately."

"Why not?" Zet and Kat said at the same time.

"Look at me, I could never walk to the other end of Thebes like this. It's too far. And besides—"

Moss shot past, shouting and holding a wooden horse high overhead, with Akiki and Sefu in pursuit.

"As you can see, it would be difficult, to say the least," she said with a laugh.

"But you have to go," Zet said.

"He'll be expecting you," Kat cried. "He hasn't seen his family for six months. And it's not like he's in another city, he's right here. Think of how sad he'll be if you don't show up."

"Exactly." Zet crossed his arms over his chest. "I bet he'll be the only kid without a visitor."

At this, Delilah's cheeks flushed. Zet cringed, regretting his last comment.

"I'll stay here," Kat said, "And babysit."

"And you can lean on me," Zet said. "I'll help you walk there."

Some adults might have gotten mad at them by now. But Delilah wasn't like most adults. She threw her arms in the air.

"You kids will be the end of me," she cried. "But fine. All right. I'll go."

"Yippee!" Zet said.

"And I'm going to do it in style. I'm going to hire a litter to carry me." She held her belly with one hand. "The gods know I don't indulge in luxury much. So why not?" She smiled, but then looked suddenly concerned. "I don't know, though, Kat. Are you sure you're up for the chaos?"

"Of course," Kat said, and gulped.

Zet was relieved as they worked out the details. They left Hui's house and headed home. Soon, he'd get to see Hui. Then he'd know for certain what was going on.

CHAPTER 5
HOME

Back home, the delicious scent of dinner met them as they opened the door. Zet's stomach made a ferocious growl.

Kat laughed.

Having skipped lunch, he was starved. "I could eat a hippo."

"Gross," Kat said. "I bet it would be really chewy."

At this, he grinned.

"Dinner's on the table," their mother called.

Moments later, the whole family was seated on cushions—Zet, Kat, their mother and baby brother, Apu. They didn't talk. They were too busy stuffing their mouths. Their mother had splurged and made a roast goose, along with a salad of sliced fennel and onions in a tangy lemon dressing. For dessert, there were soft, ripe dates stuffed with honey roasted almonds.

Finally, Zet groaned and leaned back, full.

"That was so good."

"Long day?" their mother said, smiling and clearly pleased at his enjoyment of her cooking.

Zet nodded, his mind roaming to his problems at the stall. He and Kat hadn't told their mother about the angry customers, and how the pottery hadn't arrived. They didn't want to worry her. But it had come to the point where he needed her advice. She knew the people at the pottery guild better than he did. She'd been there often, first with their father, and more recently with Zet and Kat.

"There's something I wanted to ask you about," Zet said.

He glanced at Kat, who bit her lip.

"What is it?" their mother said. "Is something wrong?"

Zet began to explain. It all came tumbling out in a rush; how the orders had been placed and paid for by the women, how Zet had paid the potters with their remaining savings, and how the orders hadn't come.

"We'll have to repay the women," Zet said.

"And they're spreading terrible rumors," Kat added. "People might stop buying from us. And everyone in the market is angry with us, too. We might even lose the stall."

"I wish you'd told me earlier," their mother said. "It's getting so close to the festival."

"I know . . . we just, I thought we could handle it," Zet said, coloring.

"Oh dear." She looked upset. Worried. She stood abruptly and carried the dishes to the kitchen.

Zet and Kat hurried to clear the rest.

"Well," their mother said. "At least you've told me. For now, you'll just have to tell the women they can choose a second set of dishes. Either they'll get their orders, or we'll deliver the second set. And when their orders do eventually come, which they will, they can keep both sets."

"Both sets," Zet gasped. "Do you realize how much—"

"That's my decision. It's better to take the loss and keep our reputation, don't you think?"

Zet nodded, mute. What good was a reputation, if they went out of business?

Kat's face had gone pale. She kept the records of trade. She knew they could never afford that.

"Don't worry." Their mother pulled them both close. "It will all work out." She kissed the top of their heads. "My guess is the shipment will arrive in the morning. You two go to work, and I'll take Apu on a little outing to where the pottery guild docks their boat. If they're not there, I'll find out what's happened. All right?"

Zet let out a huge sigh. "Okay."

A short time later, Zet climbed the ladder to the roof. He and Kat liked to sleep up there on hot nights. He lay down on his pallet and stared up at the river of twinkling stars.

Somewhere in the distance, a jackal howled. Hairs prickled along Zet's arms. Usually, the vicious animals didn't come into the city. It had to be lost. Or maddened. Or crazy.

Or possessed by Anubis, the jackal-headed god of the underworld.

Thoughts of Hui and Snaggletooth and the angry women swirled in his head.

He groaned and rolled over, and soon fell into a restless sleep.

In his dreams, a pair of wild jackals with glowing red eyes chased him into a dead end. The two animals were huge, with slathering teeth. Cornered, Zet tried to climb to freedom. The walls were slippery.

He was trapped.

IIe had to get out!

The two jackals inched closer and closer, eyes like flaming coals, enjoying his panic.

CHAPTER 6
CHILLING NEWS

The following day dawned bright and hot.

On their way to work, Zet and Kat passed dozens of unusually silent people sweeping and polishing door-handles, and burning fragrant incense cones to perfume the air. Everyone liked to spruce up their homes and entrances for the Opet Festival. The city's stone streets gleamed as they always did at this time of year.

Despite that, it felt as if an unseen darkness hung over the city.

And the dark feeling had nothing to do with Zet and Kat's problems.

People were acting downright strange. He passed a man painting a protection symbol on his front door, and chanting what sounded like a spell. Had he heard the jackal in the city last night, too?

Farther along, a woman opened her door and peeked left and right before stepping outside with her marketing basket. Her fingers clutched the handle so tightly, her knuckles looked white.

Zet shot Kat a questioning look. She shrugged.

"Weird," she whispered.

But that wasn't as weird as the sight that met them when they first entered their marketplace. A new stall stood near the entrance. The stall owner was a stooped man, with thick black hair and large, bloodshot eyes. Protection amulets of every kind swung from his awning. There were oil lamps with strange symbols Hyksos spirits probably; heady, acrid-smelling incense burned, and he was stirring liquid in a pot and chanting.

The chant sounded a lot like the one the man had been chanting outside his door.

"Who are you?" Zet asked, approaching. "What is all this stuff?"

The man's bulging eyes fastened on Zet. "I am Akar. And it is well that you ask, my boy," he said. "I take it you haven't heard the news."

"What news?" Zet said.

A slow, oily smile spread over Akar's features. "An evil army of spirits is coming."

"An evil army of spirits?" Kat gasped. "What kind of evil army of spirits?"

Zet frowned at the bug-eyed man.

"The dead souls of Hyksos invaders!" Akar said.

"That's ridiculous," Zet said.

"Is it? Already, they're creeping into town. Stirring up trouble. Casting dark dreams. Can't you feel it, children?"

"No. I can't," Zet said. But he suddenly remembered his jackal dream.

Kat grabbed Zet's wrist and whispered, "Maybe that's why our pottery hasn't come. And why Hui's acting so strange."

Zet turned to the bug-eyed man. "And what are these spirits supposedly doing?"

"My boy, don't you know? There have been thefts. A large number of them. They're stealing scarab amulets. All the golden, jeweled ones they can find. And you know how important scarabs are to Egypt. They ensure long life. They ensure birth. Creation. Balance. Be afraid. Very afraid."

Zet glared at him. "A spirit army, stealing golden scarabs? Sounds more like a jewel thief to me."

"Careful," Akar said. "And stay out of the streets at night."

Zet took Kat's elbow, before she could hear any more. It was exactly the kind of stuff she'd believe. He propelled her across the square.

"Come on, we have to open up," he said.

"But Zet—" she said.

"You're the most logical person I know. So why do you fall for all that stuff?"

"It could be true. The Hyksos spirits probably are mad. And you know they can't be burying the enemy Hyksos soldiers properly, with the war going on. They're not going to the afterlife. They're restless, and wandering, and want revenge. And what better time to take revenge than now? During the festival? When tons of people are in town, and Pharaoh and the royal family plan to make their procession and everything."

Zet grimaced. He hadn't thought of that.

"I'm not saying it's not possible," Zet said. "But there could be dozens of explanations for the scarab thefts. A spirit army is the last one I'd worry about."

As they made for their stall, Zet considered paying a visit to the medjay police.

Merimose, the head medjay, had become a friend. Zet had helped him solve the Mystery of the Missing Scroll, and had even earned a reward for doing so. It didn't mean Merimose would share restricted information, but there was a chance Zet could learn more about the thefts.

Because at the mention of stolen jewels, even though he hadn't said it out loud, his mind had gone right to Hui and the Kemet jewelry workshop.

Maybe he could escape and drop by the station for a few moments sometime during the day.

When they got to the stall, he realized there would be no time. As soon as they opened up, things got busy. Customers jammed the square. Zet and Kat had to focus on sales. And maintaining the shreds of their dying reputation.

If nothing else, tomorrow was the day he'd be visiting Hui. At least then he'd be able to see his best friend in person. He doubted Kat's crazy fears that Hui had been hypnotized, or worse, possessed. But he did want to know why Hui had pretended not to recognize her, and why Snaggletooth had attacked Zet just for asking about him.

That evening, they headed home, hoping to hear good news from their mother.

Zet prayed in silence, all the way. *Please, let her have found out about the shipment.*

Instead of good news, however, they found her packing.

"Where are you going?" Zet and Kat cried.

"Down river, to find out what went wrong."

"But right now?" Kat said, looking frightened.

Zet knew Kat was worried about being left in the city with the demon army coming.

Their mother nodded. "I know you can manage on your own. I'm leaving with baby Apu at sunrise tomorrow."

CHAPTER 7
UNDERWAY

T he next morning fell on a market-closing day. It was still dark when Zet and Kat saw their mother off at the dock.

"You were lucky to find a boat, Ma'am," said the steersman who helped her on board. "Everyone is hired out because of the festival."

"But you weren't?" Zet asked him.

"I was, but fortunate for you, the fellow who hired me canceled. Now don't you kids worry, I'll take good care of your mother here," he said.

The man leapt into the boat, cast off the ropes and poled the boat away from shore. Moments later, their mother and baby Apu looked tiny as they waved goodbye and disappeared in the river traffic.

A flash of sunlight shot over the horizon, painting the world red.

"We better run if we want to get to Hui's house on time," Zet said.

As the sun rose higher, so did his mood. Finally, they were putting an end to the stall's problems. His mother would get to the bottom of this, he was sure of it. Meanwhile, in a short while, he'd get to see Hui, and all his questions would be answered.

He and Kat were grinning and laughing by the time they reached Hui's house.

A fancy looking litter rested on the street just outside the door. It was made of two long poles, with a covered seating area in the middle, and linen drapes on either side. Two large men in leather sandals stood waiting next to it.

"Sorry we're late," Zet shouted, spotting Delilah.

Delilah's eyes were twinkling. "Not to worry. I knew you'd come. Shall we go?"

And so they were off, leaving Kat with a houseful of three rowdy boys.

Zet trotted after the two men and their swaying contraption, letting the litter bearers lead the way.

Despite the heat, the two men moved with a minimum of effort. Their breath flowed in regular rhythm. Their footsteps made a light patter. Only a telltale line of sweat down the closest man's back showed how much work was involved in holding Delilah steady. High on their shoulders, the litter seemed to almost float down the street. A very pregnant Delilah, meanwhile, lounged like royalty amongst the pillows.

The small group cut down twisting back streets. Zet was shown all sorts of shortcuts through the city.

After thirty minutes or so, they reached the edge of the artisan quarter. The tannery with its foul smells greeted them with such force that Delilah coughed in the acrid air and Zet shielded his nose and mouth with his arm.

Further on, he glanced sideways through an open door, into a room that glowed red and billowed heat. Inside, a man stood next to a forge, banging a long metal blade into shape over a stone. Zet slowed to watch. The roof was open to the sky. Sparks wound upward, twirling into the morning air.

He was falling behind, and ran to catch up to the litter.

The delicious aroma of baking bread stopped him short. He spotted the bakeshop and his stomach roared. Beyond a curtained entryway, plump loaves of date-studded bread stood on open shelves. He loved date bread.

"Here we are, madam," said one of the litter bearers.

Zet spun to see them put the litter down. They were there? Then he realized that they really had reached the Kemet Workshop.

But it looked different.

A bright carpet had been laid at the entrance. Two slim male servants stood to greet them. They were expensively dressed: blinding white tunics, a large turquoise pin at each man's shoulder, gold bands on their wrists, and braided reed sandals. Only the tattoos on the palms of their hands marked them as Kemet's servants.

There was no sign of Snaggletooth. As for the horrible black gate with its creepy, knife-like points on top—well, it was hidden in shadow. All pressed back against the inner wall, so no one could see.

Zet stared.

"You are here to visit an apprentice, my lady?" the nearest servant asked.

"My son, Hui," Delilah said.

"Then welcome to you. Please, let me help you," he said.

"Thank you." Delilah took his hand and stepped out onto the carpet. She'd brought a sack of things for Hui, and reached down to lift it out.

"I'll take that for you," the closest servant said.

"Don't worry yourself, I can manage."

"As you wish, my lady," the servant said, and bowed. There was a note of disapproval in his voice, as if he thought her coarse for wanting to carry her own bag. "Please, enter."

Clearly excited at the promise of seeing Hui, Delilah moved past him, into the narrow entrance.

Zet started to follow, but the servant sprang in front of him with surprising speed. The man stretched out both gold-braceleted arms and barred Zet's way.

"I'm with her," Zet said.

"You are Hui's brother?"

"His best friend."

"It is not allowed."

CHAPTER 8

AN UNWELCOMING

Zet's hands unconsciously formed into fists as he stared in surprise at the servant blocking his way.

"What do you mean, it's not allowed?" Delilah said. "He's with me."

The servant frowned. "As I said—"

"I heard what you said, young man. Where's Kemet?"

"Madam, please. Those are the rules."

"I want to speak to Kemet. Immediately."

"Madam! But he's—"

"Now." Delilah was usually the kindest, gentlest person around. But threaten anyone close to her and she turned into a lioness. Her cheeks had turned that angry shade of red that meant someone was about to be in big trouble. Zet, Kat and Hui were all terrified of that look. Her being pregnant didn't help matters.

The servant shuffled his feet, and glanced at the man next to him.

"Young man, did you not hear me?" Delilah said.

"Hear what?" came a pleasant voice from the dark doorway beyond.

Everyone turned as a man emerged from the shadows. He was a

little shorter than average, and laugh lines radiated around his gray-blue eyes.

"What's seems to be the trouble, my lady?"

"I want to speak with Kemet."

"I am he."

Zet stared. It was the man in the boat! The rich man who'd been speaking to Hui.

Today Kemet wore an expensive looking gold-bordered tunic, but on close inspection, it was clear he'd seen a lot of hard work. Burn scars dotted his arms and wrists, no doubt from melting and shaping hot metal. Zet's eyes went to Kemet's fingers and he stifled a gasp.

Kemet may have worked hard once, but he couldn't make jewelry anymore; the craftsman's hands were swollen and curled into useless, gnarled claws.

Ignoring Zet, Kemet's smile widened as he approached.

"Welcome to you, my lady. And how may I be of assistance?"

Delilah wrapped her arms around herself. "I'm Delilah. I'm here to visit my son, and your servant won't let my companion in."

"I see. And this is your companion?" he asked, nodding at Zet.

"Yes. Zet's like a son to me. And I brought him to help me." She clutched one hand to her belly. "Not that I should even have to explain. What kind of place is this?"

Kemet laughed. "I see you've never visited a jeweler's workshop before. We simply need to be cautious given the wealth of materials we handle. But come in, both of you." He waved them forward. "This way."

The servant scowled at Zet and took up his post at the gate once again.

Turning his back on him, Zet followed the crippled owner. All was silent as they headed for the shadowed door at the far end of the narrow entranceway. When they reached it, Kemet stood back and let them enter.

Zet found himself in a cool, dark hallway. He squinted, waiting for his eyes to adjust.

"I'm going to assume you're trustworthy," Kemet said, close at his elbow.

"I don't even have pockets," Zet said. "Even if I wanted to steal something. Which I don't."

"You'd be surprised at the creative way people have of hiding things. But enough of that unpleasant topic. All our boys are in the forecourt. They're quite excited to have the day off," Kemet said, leading them ahead. "Hui is eager to see you, my lady."

"Is my son happy here?" Delilah asked.

"Very. He's my star-apprentice," Kemet said.

She flushed and smiled. "Really?"

"He's the best I've ever seen."

It was clear Kemet meant it. Zet couldn't help feeling impressed.

They passed an open door. Inside, Zet spotted forges blackened with use. In the next room, racks of shelves held a dizzying array of tools. Further, he glanced into a room and saw dozens of shelves stacked with stoppered containers of various sizes.

Kemet was suddenly at his side. "Like I said, expensive materials." He waved at the jars. "Those contain jewels and precious metals."

"Oh. Why is the door open?"

"To let our guests see the workshop. Normally we keep it locked."

"A guest could take something."

He shrugged. "It's a risk."

This seemed weird. Totally out of line with Kemet's earlier worry. They kept walking, and Zet suddenly noticed a small, narrow slot in the wall. It was so well placed, he only spotted it because something moved in the darkness beyond the hole and caught his eye.

Were they being watched?

He noticed more slots as they made their way down the corridor.

He walked past one, pretending to ignore it. At the last second, he turned, spun, and looked directly through the hole. He caught the whites of someone's eyes.

Then nothing.

It was downright creepy.

They were definitely being watched.

Was it like this all day long? The idea of having eyes on him all the time made him shudder. He couldn't wait to hear what Hui said about it.

CHAPTER 9
THE KEMET WORKSHOP

"Now, it's Zet isn't it?" Kemet asked, turning to him. "What about you, boy? You're not apprenticed anywhere?"

"I work for my family."

"I see."

"Oh, Zet's being modest," Delilah said with a laugh. "He runs the most popular pottery stall in Thebes."

"Indeed? You're an artist then? You make earthenware?" Kemet asked.

"Actually, no. We buy our wares from a potters' guild downriver."

"Well, we can't all be artists," Kemet said with a laugh.

Zet frowned.

"Zet might not be an artist, but he has some special talents," Delilah said. "He solves crimes. Isn't that right, Zet?"

"I guess," Zet answered with a shrug. It was the last thing he wanted to talk about, even if Kemet seemed friendly. He didn't want to put the man on guard. "Where's the forecourt?" he asked, trying to change the subject. "Are we almost there?"

"Nearly," Kemet said. But he wouldn't be thrown off so easily. "What are these crimes you've solved?"

"Nothing really. It's not that interesting."

"Not interesting?" Delilah stopped. "Zet, you saved Pharaoh's life!"

"Pharaoh?" Kemet stopped to look at him. "Indeed. Now that is something I find very interesting."

Delilah said, "Zet stopped a group of criminals from sneaking into the palace. They were going to kill Pharaoh. The city police—the medjay—even gave Zet a reward. Isn't that right, Zet?"

Kemet was watching Zet's face.

Zet shrugged. "Luck."

Kemet studied him with eyes like a serpent—cold, calculating and deadly. After a moment, he said, "Luck only favors the skilled."

Then the jeweler turned and walked quickly toward a sunny, open door.

Zet swallowed and glanced at Delilah. She didn't seem to notice anything strange in the man's behavior.

Together, they stepped from the cool hallway into the blistering light of a walled courtyard.

"The forecourt," Kemet said, gesturing.

Zet blinked in the brightness, scanning the crowded outdoor area. Tables held groups of people chatting in excited voices. It was easy to spot the trainees—each one wore a tunic with Kemet Apprentice stitched in gold hieratic script.

It took a moment to spot Hui. Then he saw him. In the farthest corner, away from the crowd, Hui sat at a table beneath a shaded awning.

Hui looked shocked to see Zet.

Zet watched his best friend quickly cover his surprise.

"Hui," Delilah cried. One hand on her belly, she waddled at almost a run.

Zet followed more slowly. A guard stood in the corner, no more than ten paces from Hui. He had his arms crossed over his bare, barrel-shaped chest.

Snaggletooth.

The huge guard turned and spotted Zet. Zet hoped the thug wouldn't recognize him, but he was out of luck. Snaggletooth's lip curled up on one side in an ugly grin. He bent his thick, muscled arm like he was grabbing Zet in a chokehold, and flexed his bicep.

Was that supposed to be a joke? If so, it wasn't funny.

Zet kept his face like a stone mask and walked the last few paces to his friend. He wouldn't give Snaggletooth the satisfaction of seeing how freaked out he was inside.

Hui had his arms around his mom. Which wasn't easy, given the size of her belly. Still, he squeezed her for a long moment before pulling away.

"Wow, I almost started to go all sappy or something," Hui said. "Guess I've been cooped up in here too long."

Hui raised his fist, and Zet bumped his knuckles like they always did. Hui certainly didn't look hypnotized, or possessed, or anything weird like that. He looked like good old Hui. Still, it was clear Zet's best friend was guarded. His eyes seemed to shoot Zet a warning —*don't mention seeing me in the boat.*

Out loud, Hui said, "I can't believe you're here."

"Ha! Same," Zet said. "It's pretty boring without you around."

Hui grinned. "What, no new terror squad's replaced us?"

"What's all this about a terror squad?" Delilah said.

"Joking, Mom. We're not a terror squad." Hui winked at Zet. "Except in Kat's mind, of course."

"That reminds me, Kat sent you something," Zet said.

He reached into a fold in his tunic for the gift Kat had sent. At the mention of Kat, Hui colored a little. It was obvious he was thinking of how he'd ignored her shouts.

"Oh?" Hui said, sounding awkward.

"Yes. She sent you a clay donkey." Zet held it out.

Taking it, Hui's mouth quirked in a grin. "A donkey, huh. Now there's a message for you." His eyes twinkled. "Let me guess, she's trying to remind me I behaved horribly. Well, tell her I apologize. And it wasn't my fault, by the way."

"No, I didn't think so," Zet said, knowing they were talking about the boat. "But you seem strangely happy about her choice in presents."

In a grand, funny voice, he said, "Tell Kat I shall treasure it forever. Hui, the donkey boy. Watch this." He ducked and shielded his mouth.

A second later, the sound of a donkey braying burst from the far hallway. Everyone turned to look. One guard even darted forward, and ran halfway to the door before he realized he'd been tricked. He stopped and glanced around slowly, narrowing his eyes. Hui wore the most innocent expression imaginable.

"Hui," Delilah said in a stern voice that barely disguised a laugh. "I hope that's not how you've been behaving!"

"Never." Hui's face was solemn.

"Humph. And somehow you're still Kemet's star apprentice." But her eyes twinkled and it was obvious Delilah was glowing with pride.

CHAPTER 10
STRANGE BUSINESS

"I should show you some of my work," Hui said. "Want to see?"

Zet and Delilah nodded. Hui unwrapped various items bundled in soft cloth.

Hui's work was incredible. Zet was seriously impressed.

There were amulets of gold, all studded with jewels. Zet thought of the new vendor in his market, and how Hui's work made those amulets look like the worst, cheapest trinkets.

"Look at this one," Delilah said with a tiny sigh. "It's beautiful."

It was a tiny gold statue of Maat, Goddess of Truth. The goddess looked ready to do her job—to greet people when they arrived in the afterlife. She'd weigh your heart against her feather, to judge if you deserved to live for all eternity.

At a prod of Delilah's finger, the scales actually moved.

"You can take the feather off of the scale," Hui said.

"Wow," Delilah said.

"It was my test project to be Kemet's new partner," Hui said, but colored suddenly.

"Kemet's partner? What do you mean?" Delilah said.

Hui laughed, nervous, as if he'd said something he shouldn't have. "Er . . . well, sorry, that just slipped out. Kemet's partner left recently, and so I'm doing some extra projects. That's all. Don't mention it to Kemet though, it's kind of a secret."

"All right," Delilah said, frowning.

As Zet took in this news and the strange expression on Hui's face, he flashed back to seeing Hui in the boat that afternoon. Were the special projects and the boat trip connected? Something strange was going on here. But what?

He glanced around, and couldn't help noticing just how many sentries there were. Several barrel-chested men per family. Huge and dark, as if they'd been baked in the same pottery mold. A shiver ran down his back.

"There sure are a lot of guards here," Zet said in a low voice.

Instantly, Hui's face changed. He still wore that good-humored look, but there was something serious underneath that only a good friend like Zet would detect.

"Oh, yeah," Hui said lightly. "That's the jewelers' business for you."

"I saw these creepy slots everywhere."

"Slots?" Delilah said.

But it was obvious Hui knew exactly what Zet meant. His eyes darted to Snaggletooth and back. "You know, all that guard stuff is boring." Hui's expression turned cold—a clear warning that Zet's probing questions were off limits.

Zet whispered, "Hui, I need to know if—"

Hui shook his head. Under his stiff smile was a look of sheer terror.

Zet picked up a wide, pectoral neck-collar made of such delicate links that it felt like fabric. "I mean, what I was wondering is, are you sure you're not pulling my leg? You really made all this stuff?"

Hui's expression changed to relief. He laughed. "Yes. And you don't have to look so shocked about it."

Zet grinned. "Okay. I guess the master trickster is allowed to be a pro at something else, too."

"What did I tell you?" Kemet said, appearing out of nowhere. "Good, isn't he?"

The crippled jeweler had come on them so swiftly and silently that Delilah nearly dropped the pendant she'd been studying.

Delilah put her hand to her chest. The jovial man smiled at her.

"My apologies," Kemet said. "I didn't mean to startle you." He gestured at Hui's work with one claw-like hand. "Impressive, isn't it?"

"Amazing," Delilah said.

"Really good," Zet agreed.

"So, what's all this about a master trickster?" Kemet asked.

Zet's best friend colored and his shoulders tightened.

Kemet had been listening in?

"Not for real," Zet said, on guard.

"I see. Then why did they call you a trickster, Hui?"

Delilah said, "Boys will be boys." She waved the topic away. "Kemet, I must say you're a wonderful teacher. I never realized he'd be doing work like this already. And I admit I've been worried about the workshop being so off-limits, but now I see it's having a good effect on my son. Hui seems very grown up."

"Mother, thanks. I'm sitting right here," Hui said.

Kemet barked out a laugh. "So you are, my young friend. I can teach until I'm blue in the face, but takes a good student to actually learn." The wrinkles around his eyes deepened. "Still, a trickster? Now that's news. I enjoyed playing a joke or two when I was young." He grinned. "These visitor days are good for us as well as the families. We find out all sorts of things about our boys."

The statement hung for a moment.

Kemet bowed. "I must move on to the next group. Lunch will be served shortly. Enjoy."

"It's nice he's so proud of you. I'm proud of you, too." Delilah hugged her son. "I'm so glad we came today."

"Me, too," Hui said. Still in her arms, he shot Zet a meaningful glance.

But as to what he meant by it, Zet had no idea.

What was going on here? They needed to talk, but how?

Still, it didn't make sense. Why would Hui be in danger? This was a proper business, a workshop. And he was Kemet's star pupil.

CHAPTER 11

QUESTIONS WITH NO ANSWERS

On their way to lunch, they detoured by the sleeping quarters. Zet hoped they could talk as they walked, but his hopes were cut short. Snaggletooth followed a few paces behind.

"My domain," Hui said, showing him the small cell he shared with another boy.

A sleeping pallet lay against either wall.

"That one's mine," Hui said.

Next to Hui's pallet, a table was heaped with possessions. In the middle, overseeing Hui's collection of things, stood a statue of Bes—Hui's family god. Grinning troublemaker himself. The funny little dwarf god fit Hui's zany family perfectly. Sure, he protected their household, like all family gods did, but Bes also loved to stir up trouble. Generally of the entertaining kind. It was no wonder Hui loved joking around.

At Bes's feet lay a half burned cone of incense. Beside that lay a big old hippo's tooth.

"You still have that?" Zet said.

"Of course."

"Remember when you found it?" Zet said.

"After nearly losing my foot to an angry old croc? Yes." Hui laughed.

"I think that's the last time Kat went swimming in the Nile," Zet said, grinning. "But I still don't believe there was a croc after you."

"It was under the water, all right. Why do you think I leapt out, screaming?"

"Uh—to scare the living ka out of Kat?"

"Would I do that?" Hui said, all innocent.

"Definitely."

Hui cut in on Zet's thoughts. "Before you leave, don't let me forget I have gifts for you." He hauled a sack out from a trunk. "And don't say you don't want them. But you can look at them later. When you get home." He held the sack close to his chest. "Now let's go eat."

"I want to open them here, with you," Delilah said.

A sheen of sweat appeared on Hui's forehead. "No, really. Let's go, mother."

"Whatever you like," she said.

Lunch was served in a smaller, adjoining courtyard. Finely made spoons, carved of out ivory, lay at each place. Holding his spoon up, Zet could see the light through it.

"I hope I don't break this thing by eating with it," Zet said.

"Which is why I'm going for the bread option," Hui said, tearing off a piece. Using it like a spoon, he scooped up a bite full of thick, rich stew, and shoved his mouth full.

Zet copied him. "Good bread."

Hui's face was bent over his food. "They make it next door," he said, speaking into his dish.

Zet spent the rest of the meal trying to think up ways to communicate with Hui.

Hui looked pained, as if he was trying to figure the same thing.

But it was impossible. There were people and guards all around.

The meal finished way too fast. And then the visitors were all being politely, but efficiently, ushered toward the door. People were saying good-bye, hugging, telling their boys to write.

There was a line to get outside. They filled the narrow entryway that led to the outer gate. Zet, Hui and Delilah craned to see what was going on. Ahead, a family stood talking to the servants who'd first greeted them when they arrived.

"We need to check your bags," one of the servants said.

The father of the family shrugged and put his belongings on a table for inspection.

Zet glanced at Hui. His best friend's cheeks had gone pale. His eyes had turned to pinpoints, watching the search. He still carried the bag of gifts, and Zet noticed his hands were trembling.

CHAPTER 12
SEARCHED

Zet's heart had begun to race. What was in that bag that made Hui so nervous?

The servant at the door motioned to the three of them. "Come forward, we're ready for you," he said. "Please, put your belongings on the table."

Delilah shot him a look of distaste. Clearly she hadn't forgotten their earlier run in with the man, when he'd tried to stop Zet from entering.

"This all seems a bit over the top," she said.

"Sorry. Routine check."

Annoyed, Delilah asked, "Why, by the gods, would we take anything?"

"Those are the procedures, madam, unless you want to leave the bag behind."

"It's fine," Hui said. His face showed nothing as he handed it over. "Just the gifts I made. The materials I used are all recorded in the daily log."

The servant referred to a sheet of papyrus. He moved his finger down the line of text, read what had been written, and reached into the sack. He pulled out several parcels, all wrapped in linen. Then he started to unwrap them.

Hui swallowed, and let out a little laugh. "I guess your presents won't be a surprise."

"That's all right," Delilah said.

The first contained a tiny kitten pendant carved of jade on a thin gold chain.

"For Kat, obviously," Hui said.

Everyone knew she loved animals, especially homeless strays. She was always putting out water and food for them in their street.

There were little trinkets for his baby brothers and something for his mother. For Zet he'd made a perfectly round ball out of polished ivory. It was large, and a wadjet eye had been carved on the surface. It was the moon, ruler of the stars. Like the spoons at lunch, the ivory looked breakable. But Zet couldn't wait to put it on display back home.

"Wow," Zet said. "That's for me?"

"Thought you'd like it," Hui said.

The servant rolled it around in his hands, checking to see if it opened.

"Careful. It's fragile," Hui said sharply.

"Don't worry, I'm taking care," the servant said. Still, his tattooed hands treated it more carefully. Deciding it didn't open, he replaced it in its covering and set it aside. Then he turned the empty satchel upside-down and shook it.

Hui pulled Zet back a few steps. "Don't worry if you break the ball. It's yours. Really. I won't be offended."

"I won't break it."

"Really. I don't mind."

"Okay," Zet said with a laugh.

Still, it was funny because Hui knew he was good at handling fragile things. He did it all day long in his stall, with the earthenware. And maybe he wasn't good at math and writing like his sister Kat, or at creative things like Hui with his metalwork and pranks, but he was good at others. Like being quick and incredibly agile. If something fell, he'd catch it, sometimes even if he were across the room. He could dive like a hawk, and land like a panther.

Well, so his mother said anyway. And he liked to think it was true.

"Wish we could've talked," Zet said so quietly that it was little more than his lips moving. "It's like we were under guard all day."

"I know."

"When are they going to let up on you?"

"Tell Kat I liked the donkey."

"The donkey?" Zet sensed someone behind him. "Oh, right. Yeah, I will. And she said to say hi to you." He turned to see Kemet. That man could sneak around like a desert breeze. How had he come up on them like that?

"I came to say good bye," Kemet said. "Thanks for visiting. I'll take good care of my star apprentice here."

At the table, the servant finished putting everything back in the bag.

"You're all clear," he said.

It was only then that Hui seemed to relax. Was something in the bag? There couldn't be. The man had checked it thoroughly. So why had Hui seemed so tense?

"Have a nice trip home," Kemet said.

Hui hugged his mother and Zet. The gate was closed between them. Delilah climbed back into the waiting litter.

The visit was over.

CHAPTER 13
A PLAN

All the way back to Delilah's, Zet puzzled over Hui's reaction to having the bag searched.

He stopped in with her to find Kat and the boys playing a game of hide and seek. At the mention of gifts, Hui's brothers cheered. They ran around with their little prizes, holding them in triumph. Kat screamed with delight over her kitten pendant.

Zet, meanwhile, took the empty bag and searched it again himself. Nothing.

"We'd better get going," Zet said to Delilah.

Delilah's cheeks were rosy "Thanks for everything," she said. "Especially for twisting my arm. And Kat, for taking care of the boys."

"It was fun," Kat said.

"Are you sure you won't stay for dinner?"

"Mother left food for us," Kat said. "We'd better eat it or she won't be too happy with us."

Moments later, they were out the door. Zet almost ran the short distance home.

"What's the hurry?" Kat called.

"I'll tell you when we get there."

Inside, he closed the front door, went to the low dining table, sat on a cushion and pulled out the ivory ball.

"What is that?" Kat said.

"I'm not sure. Hui made it for me, but I think it must open or something." He started to examine the surface, bending close. "Bring a lamp, would you?"

"Hello, I'm not your servant," Kat grumbled.

Zet rolled his eyes. "Do you want me to tell you what happened over there?"

"Yes."

"Then bring the lamp. Oh, forget it, I'll get it myself."

But Kat was already pulling it from a cubby. She filled it with oil. Meanwhile, Zet told her everything that had happened. About the spying slots, and the guards, and being searched, and how Hui was sweating when they emptied the bag of gifts.

With the lamp glowing brightly, she sank down beside him.

"So he's not possessed?"

"No," Zet said, laughing. He turned the ball over in his hands. "This thing is pretty heavy."

"Do you think there's something inside?" she asked.

"I don't know. The servant who searched the stuff tried to open it, but couldn't figure out how to do it." He held it up to the light. "But the shell is kind of sheer, and it looks like there's something in there."

He gave it a shake, holding it next to his right ear. It didn't rattle. Instead, a soft, shifting noise came from inside. Like something padded moving back and forth. He placed it on the table. Upon closer study, it became clear the ball had been crafted out of four separate pieces. The seams were so perfect, however, they were almost invisible.

Zet grasped it with both hands. Carefully, he tried twisting it this way and that. He tried pulling outward. He tried pushing on the seams, to see if that would pop it apart.

"I don't get it," he muttered.

Lifting the ball again, he studied the wadjet eye etched in the center.

"Try pushing on that," Kat said.

He did. Nothing happened.

"It doesn't open," he said.

"Maybe the eye is supposed to mean something?" she said, doubtful.

He scratched his head; he'd shaved it recently, and the stubble still felt strange and prickly. "This is so frustrating! I was there. I talked to Hui. And I still have no idea what's going on. But I know something's going on, Kat."

She fingered her jade kitten pendant. "Maybe."

"What are you thinking? What's that look?"

Kat bit her lip. "Well, I was just thinking, maybe something's going on, or maybe it has to do with the demon army that's—"

"Stop right there," Zet said. "This has nothing to do with some demon army. Hui's in trouble. And this ball isn't telling me anything. I need to talk to him. In private."

"I don't see how you're going to do that," Kat said.

Zet wrapped the ball back up and carefully stored it away.

"I do," Zet said. He went to the ladder that led to the roof, and clambered up the wooden rungs. Outside, the wind moved easily across the rooftops, cooling the evening air. A welcome breeze ruffled his tunic. Laundry rustled on a line, giving off the sharp, floral scent of natron mixed with lavender. From further off, he caught the faint, briny scent of the Nile, which flowed in the distance.

Turning his back on the Nile, he glanced toward the far away artisan quarter.

The sun god dipped toward the horizon.

"It's too early, still," he said, hearing Kat join him on the roof.

"Too early for what?"

"To pay Hui a visit."

"You don't mean—are you saying you're going to sneak in?" Kat gasped.

"Hui would do it for me."

Kat nodded. "All right. But we should eat something first. It's a long way, and you've already walked it once."

"We? You're not coming," Zet said.

"I am, and don't even think about trying to stop me. I'll just follow you. I can find my way there myself, anyway."

Zet groaned. Why had he said anything? The last thing he needed was Kat tagging along. An ebony colored cat met his eyes from a windowsill across the way. If he expected the cat to look sympathetic, he was disappointed. The cat flicked its tail and disappeared.

"You'll just get us in trouble," he said.

But there was no arguing with her, and he knew it.

CHAPTER 14

UNDER A BLACK SKY

A sliver of moon cast an eerie glow through the window. Zet opened the front door. Overhead, stars twinkled like pinpricks in a thick, black cloak.

"Time to go," Zet.

"Wait," Kat said.

Zet turned. Kat stood knotting her hands.

"Changed your mind?" he asked.

"No, it's just—" She swallowed. "Well, you heard what that new vendor, Akar, said. About going out at night. What about the demon army?"

"Good point." He nodded, sagely. "You should definitely stay here, little sister."

She frowned at him. "Oh no, you won't get rid of me that easily."

Zet let out a frustrated noise. "Look, you'll never be able to climb over the wall. And you'll make too much noise."

She glared at him. Still, her voice shook a little. "I'm coming. If you're not afraid, I'm not either."

"Ugh. Fine. But if you can't keep up, I'm leaving you behind."

"I'll keep up. I'm as fast as you."

"We'll see about that," he said, frustrated beyond belief. He knew

45

that if she couldn't keep up, he'd have to wait for her. He couldn't just leave her in the street in the middle of the night, even if that's exactly what he felt like doing right now.

They headed out the door and padded softly through the dead city.

It wasn't the first time they'd snuck through Thebes in the middle of the night, but that didn't make it any less eerie. The moon was only half full, so he had to squint just to see. In the narrower lanes, no light came in at all.

They'd walked in tense silence for at least twenty minutes when something small and soft brushed his ankle. A cat.

Kat let out a yelp. It must have brushed past her, too.

He yanked her behind a potted palm. She was shaking all over, and he knew it had nothing to do with fears of humankind.

"Quiet," he whispered. "Demons aren't furry. It was just a cat."

"Sorry," she said, trembling.

"Last thing we need is some adult finding us. There will be all sorts of questions about what we're doing and we'll never get there."

"Okay, I get it," she whispered back.

Together, they carried on. Zet had decided to follow the route the litter-bearers had taken. But now, he realized, that was a stupid idea. The first shortcut, Zet found easily. But now he was less certain of his surroundings. It felt like they'd been walking for over an hour. They probably had been.

"Are we almost there?" Kat whispered.

He groaned. "I knew I shouldn't have brought you."

"I'm just wondering because I'm lost."

"Well I'm not," he lied. Not completely.

"Didn't we pass that door before?" Kat said.

Zet walked faster. "The place is around here somewhere. Just come on. Hurry up!"

But the further they went, the more turned around he became. Soon, he was completely lost. He had no idea where they were.

"Okay stop. Stop for a second," he said.

Kat sank down against a wall.

He rubbed a hand over his face, trying to figure out which way the moon should be if they were going in the right direction. But of course the moon moved across the sky, and who knew how long they'd been walking?

Great. Some plan. Wander all night and never find the workshop because he'd decided he'd be clever and follow some stupid shortcuts. At least she didn't say anything, like how dumb he was. He sure felt it.

"What's that smell?" Kat said. "It reeks around here."

"Does it?" Zet sniffed. "It does, kind of, doesn't it?" Suddenly, he leapt to his feet. "The tannery! We must be near the tannery. We have to be close, then. Come on."

"It's stronger this way," Kat said.

Zet put a hand over his nose. "Phew, that's for sure."

"It stinks like old donkey urine," Kat said, giggling.

"You would know."

"Would not," Kat cried.

"Look, I recognize that water well." Zet pointed to its bucket, outlined in the moonlight. "We're almost there."

A few moments later, they reached it. They stopped in a shadow across the street.

Beside him, Kat studied the Kemet Workshop's locked, barbed gate.

"Creepy," she whispered.

He nodded, and whispered, "Still want to come in?"

Kat eyed him nervously. "Of course I'm coming in."

"Let's try to find a way in at the back of the complex," he said.

They skirted around the bakery, which stood to the right of the Kemet Workshop. He figured he'd find a wall all around the complex. Instead, what he found were dozens of tiny businesses. They'd grown up around the jeweler's complex, like thick bushes around the base of a giant tree. The tiny businesses blocked any passage to the workshop's wall.

Still, Zet stuck close as he made a circuit of the clump of buildings.

There had to be an opening somewhere.

There just had to be a way in.

CHAPTER 15
FOUL ENTRY

"What's this?" Zet whispered. "Look, I think we found something."

It was a narrow alley filled with refuse. A wooden fence blocked the entrance to the alley. The alley looked like a long one, and he had no doubt it led all the way to the Kemet workshop.

He rattled the fence. Locked. Still, it looked easy to climb. Not that anyone in his right mind would. It was disgusting on the other side. Piled deep with meat bones, eggshells, old paintbrushes, broken tools, and slimy old vegetables. You name it. All decomposing in a mountainous, rotting heap.

"Gross," Kat said.

"Exactly. Do you want to wait?"

"You're going in there?"

"Yep." He looked at her face and grinned. "Guess you're not so heroic now, huh?"

She put her fists on her hips. "I didn't say that."

"Then come on."

Holding his breath, he gave her a leg over. Kat landed in the pile with a loud squelch. She sank into it up to her armpits, and made a noise like she was going to throw up.

"Shh," he said and hauled himself over the fence after her.

The squishy mess was soft, and he sank deep. He crawled for higher ground, and then buried his nose in one elbow. "Worm boogers! Start walking before I hurl my guts."

"Walking?" she said. "More like crawling."

She was right. They crawled, slipped and slid over and through the reeking pile.

"Just don't look down," he said.

"Ack!" She shook a long piece of vegetable peel from her hand.

"Quiet," Zet said.

"Sorry," she whispered, and slipped.

He caught her under the arms. The ground offered no footholds and they both went down. Slime oozed. His hand gooshed into who knew what. The stench clogged his nostrils. The pile made goopy noises as he righted himself. His stomach threatened to rebel. He swallowed. It took all his control not to throw up.

Struggling to his feet, he came face to face with a glassy eyeball, staring at him out of a rotting fish head.

"Ugh," he said.

"Help me up," Kat said in a trembling voice.

He pulled her upright. "Come on, let's get up on that roof before I toss my guts."

Her chin wobbled.

"Don't you dare start crying," he warned in a furious whisper.

She swallowed, balling her fists. "This is the dumbest idea you ever had."

"No," he whispered back. "You're coming with me was the dumbest idea I ever had."

They reached where the alley dead-ended at a wall. He gave her a leg up onto the roof above. Of course, she made way too much noise. Couldn't she move more quietly? They'd be killed!

Seconds later, he joined her. The roof spanned two human lengths. Then it ended at an open space.

"Let me go first," he whispered.

She nodded.

Belly down, he started forward. Hopefully he wasn't crawling over

Snaggletooth's bedroom. The thought of the scary thug staring at his ceiling, wondering what was making that shuffling noise, set Zet's hair on end.

He reached the roof's opposite edge.

Instantly, he recognized the uncovered area that opened below him. It was the courtyard where he'd met Hui earlier. This was good. He knew where he was now. And the courtyard was deserted. The table where he'd sat with Hui was gone, but he was looking straight at where it had been. All was silent. Empty. No guards in sight.

He breathed a sigh of relief and motioned to Kat.

She crawled forward on hands and knees. Just as she reached the edge, however, her arm bumped a loose piece of tile. It skittered out of reach, too far to catch. Still, Zet lunged out, as if he could draw it back. He watched in horror as it fell to the ground.

The tile landed with a crunch.

Zet yanked her back out of sight.

Wormsnot and beetledung! He was a complete idiot to bring her here. How much more noise did she plan to make?

He lay on his back, unmoving, and she did the same. Together they listened for footsteps. Someone was bound to investigate.

Sure enough, the shuffle of sandals approached and stopped directly below their hiding spot.

CHAPTER 16
FOUND

In the dead night air, Kat's fast breathing sounded like bellows. Zet squeezed her arm in warning, hard enough to hurt, and she stopped. He knew she was holding her breath. Any second she'd take a huge inhale. The guard would hear. They'd have to run for it. Back over the garbage pile. They'd never get out on time. The guard could dart out the front door and cut them off at the wooden gate.

Maybe it was Snaggletooth.

Zet's heart slammed in his ears. He stared at the sky and prayed to the gods for the guard to disappear.

Maybe the gods were listening. The footsteps died away down a corridor.

Beside him Kat gasped, like she'd been holding her breath too long.

"Stop it or he'll come back!" he said.

"I have to breathe," she hissed. "By the gods, Zet, this is crazy!"

"Stay here," he said.

"Why? What are you going to do?"

"What I came here to do. I'm going to find Hui."

"It's too dangerous."

"I didn't climb through all that garbage for nothing."

"We'll be caught." Kat's cheeks looked white with terror in the moonlight.

"Just stay flat. If anyone's going to get caught, it will be me." With that, he swung over the gutter and into the shadows of the courtyard.

Landing on silent feet, he crouched and looked both ways.

The sleeping chambers were to the right. He remembered their location from his visit. Inching slowly along, keeping his back to the wall, he reached the corridor. Zet knew he reeked. If a guard came this way, his smell alone would be enough to raise the alarm. He had to move fast.

The rooms weren't far now. He could see the dark openings.

Now all he needed was to remember which room belonged to Hui.

He counted the doors. There were a dozen on each side. Had it been the third one down? No, the fourth. Was it, though? He grimaced. He'd just have to pick one.

Aware of the tiniest sounds, he flinched at the sound of his bare feet against the paving stones. Holding his breath, he tiptoed through the third door. A tiny chink of moonlight followed him inside. A bed stood against either wall. The beds were full, the occupants breathing in a steady rhythm.

But something wasn't right.

Then he saw it. Hui's statue of his family god, Bes, was missing.

This wasn't Hui's room.

The boy on the right snorted and his arm went to his nose.

Zet stepped backward, preparing to sprint. The boy turned over and faced the wall. His breathing resumed a steady rhythm.

Back in the corridor, Zet's back prickled. He turned slowly. Someone was seated at the end of the corridor! A huge figure, with his back against the wall. Why didn't the man get up? Why didn't he say something? Zet's legs twitched, longing to flee. The man's head flopped slightly to the right and he let out a great snore.

Moonlight brushed his ugly face, turning it blue-gray.

Snaggletooth.

Cold sweat slid down Zet's ribs.

He had no choice but to try another door. Any tiny movement could wake the guard. He'd have to be smart, and fast. Moving silently, he padded to the next opening. Before entering, he squinted through the darkness and found it. Hui's statue. With a glance at Snaggletooth, he left the hallway and stepped inside.

Now he had a new problem. If he shook Hui awake, his best friend might call out. Or think he was being attacked and struggle. Snaggletooth would be there in two strides.

Zet could feel that big arm around his head, twisting until it disconnected with a sickening crunch.

Sweat prickled on his scalp.

He hadn't thought of this.

He stared at his best friend. They were several feet apart. But what could he do?

Hui solved the problem.

He sat up and stared hard at Zet. The faint light was on Hui's face. His friend looked shocked. He squinted, and Zet knew he had to be completely in shadow, silhouetted against the door. Despite that, Hui got quietly out of bed and crossed the short distance. He grabbed Zet's wrist and yanked him out the door.

With a glance at the sleeping Snaggletooth, Hui dragged him down several corridors in silence before he came to a stop.

"Are you crazy?" Hui whispered into his ear.

Zet nodded. Then he motioned for Hui to follow.

Hui put both hands over his face, as if in agony, but dropped them with a resigned groan and followed.

The boys made it to the courtyard. One after the other, they climbed onto the roof.

"Kat?" Hui whispered, seeing her there. "You, too? You're both mad. And you reek, by the way."

"We were worried," Kat said.

"It's too dangerous for you to be here."

CHAPTER 17
OUT OF TIME

Despite Hui's joking, he looked totally freaked out.

"Move back," he whispered. "Out of sight."

The three of them crawled across the clay tiles, scraping their hands and knees. Some were loose, and made shifting, clinking noises that sounded loud in the silent night. Every sound made Zet cringe. He was reminded of old times back home, but this was no game.

For once, the danger was real.

Hui stopped and Zet banged into him. Despite everything, they grinned at one another. Then Hui made a face and covered his nose.

"I'm serious," Hui said, snorting with laughter, "You guys really reek."

"You think we reek? Try crawling through your garbage pile back there. Don't they ever clean that thing out?"

"Stop joking," Kat said. "What's going on here, Hui, are you in danger?"

"That's one way of putting it," he said. "Next time I get some dumb idea to become a jeweler's apprentice, pour hot oil on my fingers or something. If there is a next time."

"What's going on? What's Kemet doing in there? Is it Kemet, or someone else?"

Footsteps sounded in the courtyard.

"Shh," Hui whispered.

They lay there, waiting.

After a long moment, Hui whispered, "The place is full of guards. They patrol all night long. If they find me missing . . ." The words trailed off as he peered through the darkness, as if trying to see below. There was no trace of the joker in Hui now. He seemed genuinely terrified.

"What would they do?" Zet whispered.

"Look, there's going to be a shipment on the first day of the festival. If you want to help, bring medjay. Have the shipment searched."

"A shipment of what? What should I tell the medjay?"

Two sets of footsteps were heading their way.

Hui jolted to his knees. "Shoot. I have to go."

"No," Zet said. "Come with us! Right now. We'll hide you."

"I'm not going to spend my life hiding out. We have to stop them."

"We will. We'll take you to the medjay right now."

"And say what? No, we have to catch them at their game. It's the only way. Look, I have to go. I can't make Kemet suspicious of me. If I'm not careful, he'll make me disappear. I know that's what happened to his partner. I heard them talking."

"His partner? You mean the one who left?"

"Yes. I don't think he left. I think they got rid of him. He screwed up, big time, and that's why everything—" Hui broke off as the clank of armed guards approached.

"He's not in his bed," growled a man. Snaggletooth.

"D'you think he's made a run for it?" said the other.

"Take the right corridor." Snaggletooth cracked his knuckles. "If he's here, we'll find him."

Zet's stomach roiled.

"Show yourself, boy," Snaggletooth called.

Hui bought a tiny moment by creating one of his famous, voice-throwing diversions. He placed his hands around his mouth and made a strange choking noise that sounded like it came from a hall in the distance.

The guards ran off after it.

Hui turned to Zet. "Look at the ball. You'll figure it out!"

"The ivory ball? I did."

"Then look again," Hui rolled off the roof and ran.

A moment later, Zet heard the scuffle of footsteps and Hui struggling.

"Caught you," Snaggletooth growled.

"Let go!" Hui said. "Can't a kid use the bathroom?"

"The bathroom is the other way."

"Well, it's dark. I got lost."

Nudging Kat, Zet said, "Time to get moving."

Her eyes were focused in the direction of the voices, and her face was pale. She nodded slowly, and then dragged her attention away from their friend. "They won't hurt him, will they?"

"Don't worry, he can handle them," Zet whispered. He just hoped it was the truth. All he could do now was leave and try to figure things out before the first day of the festival.

The sight of the refuse pit was even less welcoming the second time around.

"Let's make this fast." He jumped down into it. He wanted out so badly that he stopped trying to be careful about what he touched. He just waded through the garbage. Clearly, Kat felt the same. He glanced over his shoulder to see her propelling herself through, using her hands to scramble along.

Almost there. The gate lay just a few feet up ahead.

And then Kat screamed.

Not a quiet scream, either.

It was like a high-pitched explosion. It tore through the silence. It echoed off the stones. It filled the night sky. It had to have woken every human within shrieking distance, because the effect was instant.

Bodies could be heard slamming out of beds. Doors banged open. Footsteps hammered the ground. People were running to investigate. They'd be here in seconds.

Still, Kat kept screaming. She scrambled backward, fell under, and came up again.

Zet grabbed her and shook her hard. "Stop it. STOP IT!"

She choked into silence. Her eyes were wild.

"Move," he told her. "Quick."

She nodded. Somehow, he got her to the gate and forced her over it. He scrambled after her and landed in a crouch. Looking right, Zet spotted people coming down the street.

"There!" shouted a man who sounded a lot like Snaggletooth. "Down there, by the garbage gate."

"Run," Zet gasped. "Run or we're dead!"

White-faced, Kat turned and fled. Zet ran after her. He could hear men in close pursuit. Kat rounded a corner, black hair flying. Zet sprinted past her. He pulled her around another corner, and then another. She was starting to gasp.

"Keep going," he said.

Hauling her forward, they tore through alleys until he was completely lost. Suddenly, in a haze of horror, he saw the bakeshop. They'd made a full circle.

The gated front entryway to Kemet's Workshop gaped open, dark and menacing—like a black hole into the underworld.

Kat put her hands on her knees and bent to catch her breath. She started to sob.

"What are you doing? Don't stop!" he said.

CHAPTER 18

DEMONS

Shouts sounded in the distance. Footsteps, getting closer.

"I can't—" Kat gasped, clutching her sides.

"You have to. Come on, you can do it. Run!"

Fastening on to his sister's wrist, Zet hauled her through the darkness. He was breathing hard. The sprint combined with the struggle through the dank garbage pit was taking its toll. Still, he couldn't stop. He had to get them out of there.

"That way." He pounded through the shadows, his lungs on fire.

How long they ran, Zet had no idea.

The moon hung large and yellow over the lower walls of a temple. It glistened in the shallow, rectangular pool of water that stretched before the temple doors. They skirted around the dark, holy water. Everyone knew the temple pools were doorways into the underworld. He glanced into it, and saw shadows moving in its depths.

"Keep going," he told Kat, spooked.

"Haven't we lost them yet?" she gasped.

"Just keep going, I'll tell you when to stop."

He didn't want to lead the men to their home. He needed to be sure they'd lost them. For a moment he had a crazy notion to hide in the temple, but it was too risky. He heard footsteps in the distance, and they pressed on.

Silence surrounded them as the world slept, oblivious to Zet and Kat's terror.

He turned into a narrow lane, and then another. Suddenly, something sparkled up ahead.

"The river," he cried. "Thank the gods."

Kat sprinted alongside him, somehow finding a second wind. They reached the edge at the same time.

"That way, under the stone ledge," he said, and slipped in.

Kat didn't hover around the edge like she usually did, wading to her ankles, looking this way and that for crocodiles, water snakes, and hippos. Instead, she slipped in after him, and ducked beneath the stone overhang.

Together, they floated in silence. No one came to investigate. Still they waited, until he was sure it was safe.

They'd done it. They'd lost the guards.

Desperate to be rid of the reeking stench, Zet dove under. The water closed overhead, blissfully ending the foul smell. He floated in the darkness, letting the world and its problems disappear.

When he finally surfaced for air, Kat was still clinging to the stone overhang, but her hair was completely drenched.

With the danger gone, he felt anger well up. "What were you doing, screaming back there?"

"I didn't do it on purpose."

"You almost got us killed! And what about Hui, don't you think they're going to connect it together? Him being out, and you screaming in the garbage pit?"

She went pale. "I hadn't thought of that."

He knew she'd never get Hui in trouble on purpose. Zet felt mean about what he said. But he was mad. "Well you should've thought of it, before you woke up the whole world."

"I'm sorry," she said. "I touched . . . something. Something horrible."

"Hello—we both touched something horrible. We were in a garbage pit!"

59

"Yes, but..."

"But what?"

She covered her face. "It was awful."

Zet stared at her. "What was it? What did you touch?"

"Hands."

A chill ripped down Zet's spine. "Hands? What do you mean, hands?"

"Fingers. Grabbing me. That's what it felt like."

"Did you see them?"

"No, but I felt them, I'm sure I did."

"Fingers grabbed you? Come on. Do you hear yourself?" He was furious. Her wild imagination had nearly cost them their lives.

Kat's chin trembled. "It's the truth. Maybe it wasn't human. Maybe it was—"

He held up a hand. "Wait, don't tell me. The evil spirit army. Hiding in the pit."

She made a face. "It could have been. I felt it!"

He snorted. "I've heard enough. That's the last time I bring you with me. Ever."

With that, he pulled himself out of the water onto the stone ledge and stomped off. From behind, he heard Kat do the same.

She hurried to keep up. "What time do you think it is?"

"I don't know. Almost morning."

They'd need to be at the stall soon to open up. But first, he wanted to examine the ivory ball. Hui was in big trouble. Zet knew that now. Hopefully he could figure out what Hui meant when he'd said Zet would figure it out.

CHAPTER 19
A VISITOR

When they reached home, Zet was exhausted. Despite his urgent desire to study Hui's ball, he needed a rest. Just for a few moments. Then he'd get out the lamp and study it carefully until he knew what Hui meant.

He and Kat sank down on the cushions in the front room, too exhausted to even climb the ladder to their sleeping pallets on the roof.

He leaned back, determined not to fall fully asleep.

As soon as he closed his eyes, he drifted off.

Heat on his face made his eyes jerk open.

Sunlight streamed through the front windows.

"We're late for work," he shouted, shaking Kat awake.

Blue circles rimmed her eyes. Grotesquely colored stains splotched her tunic and her hair was matted. She was groggy, but only for a moment. In a frenzy, she tore upstairs to change. Meanwhile, Zet found himself a fresh kilt, yanked it on, and then grabbed the linen wrapped ivory ball. There was no time to find a sack. He simply carried it and ran.

"We're in trouble," Kat said. "The other vendors already think we're irresponsible."

"I know."

When they reached the market, it was in full swing. But as it turned out, Zet and Kat weren't missed. Instead, a crowd of people that included five, uniformed medjay surrounded the new amulet vendor's stall.

Akar's amulets clanked in a gentle breeze. If the man with the bulging eyes was surprised by the attention, he didn't show it. Instead, he wore a cheerful, spirited smile.

But the long established vendors weren't smiling. They were glaring. Salatis the old date-seller stood right in the middle of it all. He had his hands on his wiry hips. He and Akar seemed to be having some kind of showdown.

"We want this charlatan removed," Salatis crowed. "He's stirring up trouble for his own evil ends!"

"Not at all," said Akar. "I'm just a humble salesman, like the rest of you."

"Like the rest of us?" The fumes of some acrid potion sent Salatis into a coughing fit. He whacked his chest a few times. "Well someone knocked over all my date baskets. Right into the dirt, too. And the next thing I know, you're over at my stall telling me it was the demon army, and I should buy a protection amulet from you or it will happen again. It's fishy business!" He pointed a bony finger. "I think you knocked over my baskets, just so I'd buy something from you."

"Hold on now," boomed a familiar deep voice.

It was Merimose, the head medjay and Zet's old friend. Zet had helped him solve the case to save Pharaoh's life. Relief washed over him. He'd forgotten all about his plans to go visit the medjay. But maybe the important man could help.

Merimose was eyeing Salatis, weighing what the man said.

"You think Akar sabotaged your wares so you'd buy a magical protection device? That's a serious accusation," Merimose said. "Do you have proof?"

"No," said Salatis, "But I'm sure he did it."

"Being sure and having proof are two different things." Merimose turned to the man with the stall of magical devices. "Akar, that's your name, isn't it?"

"Yes, indeed," Akar said, grinning ear-to-ear. Clearly, the man wasn't afraid. He seemed to think all this attention was good for business. And maybe it was, because the rest of the market was empty, and crowds were pushing closer to see what was going on.

"Well, Akar, do you have papers to run this stall here?" Merimose said.

"I do indeed."

There was a lot of murmuring as the papers were studied. After a time, Merimose pronounced them good. "But I suggest you stay out of trouble," Merimose told him.

"Oh, I will, good sir. I most certainly will. Now, can I sell you a protection device of some sort? Being a police officer, you must face all sorts of terrible dangers."

Merimose laughed.

Meanwhile, Salatis and the other vendors dispersed, all of them grumbling. At the same time, the waiting crowd surged forward and started browsing Akar's stall.

"We're in the wrong business," Zet said, rolling his eyes. Then he called out, "Merimose!"

The big medjay turned. At the sight of Zet and Kat, the man's tanned, leathery face spread into a bright smile. "Thought I might see you here," he said.

"I wanted to talk to you," Zet said. "I was going to come looking for you before. Do you have a minute?"

Merimose said something to his armed men. They dispersed down various side streets, off to walk their beats.

"I better go open the stall," Kat said.

"Why don't I help you," Merimose said. "Come on, I'll give you two a hand."

One of the women who'd made special orders was waiting for them. At the sight of Merimose, she frowned.

"Well," she said, arching one brow with a satisfied look. "I'm certainly glad to see the police involved. I knew it would come to this."

Merimose shot Zet a puzzled look.

"Yes," Zet said, deciding not to correct the woman's misguided assumptions. "We're doing everything we can to track down the missing orders."

Kat led the woman away, whispering that it was best not to disturb the investigation, and that in the meantime the woman could pick a second set in case the order didn't arrive.

"Trouble?" Merimose asked Zet.

"Don't even ask."

"Very good. None of my business." Merimose picked up a clay urn. He had huge hands, like two big platters. He turned the urn around easily, even though it took Zet both arms and a few good grunts to lift it. "What's this for?"

"A beer brewing jug," Zet said.

"Huh. You learn something new every day."

He set it down with a heavy thud. His face turned serious. "Now what did you want to talk about? I've never seen you look so grim."

CHAPTER 20

THE GOLDEN SCARABS

Zet wasted no time. "Is it true that golden scarabs are being stolen from all over town?"

Furrows appeared on Merimose's tanned forehead. He rubbed the spot between his thick brows. "Where did you hear that?"

Zet shrugged. "Akar."

"Why am I not surprised?" Merimose shot a look at the busy vendor. "Well, he got it partly right. They're being stolen, but not from all over town. Just the Khonsu district."

"The Khonsu district? Where the rich people live," Zet said. "So the thieves only want expensive ones."

"Thieves always want the expensive ones, when it comes to jewelry," Merimose said with a laugh. "I suppose that's the only stuff worth stealing."

Zet nodded. Three women walked past, baskets over their arms, chatting about what they planned to cook for the upcoming Opet feast days. They stopped at Salatis's date stall across the way.

Zet lowered his voice. "So you're sure it's thieves. You don't believe it's a demon army of dead Hyksos soldiers stealing the scarabs?"

"Akar's telling people that?" Merimose said.

"Yes."

"I'm a religious man," Merimose said. "But I'm also a medjay. And where there's trouble, we usually find a living person behind it."

Zet let out a breath of relief he didn't realize he'd been holding. "That's what I thought. Still, I could see how people might believe it. It's strange the thieves aren't stealing whole jewel boxes of stuff. Why pick out only the scarabs and leave the rest?"

"That's what puzzles me too," Merimose said.

"I mean, not that I believe in the demon army," Zet said, voicing a concern he'd never admit to Kat. "But scarabs protect long life and everything. Akar says the demons are swallowing the scarabs to weaken Egypt before the Opet Festival. So we'll be unable to fend them off when they come. And the demons will come when Pharaoh and the whole city is out celebrating."

Merimose looked grim. Quietly, he said, "That's why the first person I notified, after my men, was the Head Priest."

"You notified the Head Priest?" Zet whispered, shocked.

Hearing about the demons from Akar was one thing. But from Merimose? He took the threat seriously enough to involve the priests? That was more frightening than anything Zet could imagine.

A shadow seemed to pass over the square.

"How many scarabs have been stolen?" Zet asked.

"It's hard to say," the huge medjay replied. "We've gone door to door, investigating. You'd be surprised at some of these people we've interviewed. Some of them have so many jewels they don't know what they own. And then there are mothers and sisters who are away shopping, and half of them couldn't say what the other bought recently. It's an impossible task."

"Has anyone seen the thief? You know, like running out of the house or something?"

Merimose put his big, muscular hand on the sword hilt strapped to his waist. "Not exactly."

Zet gave the man a questioning look. Merimose glanced toward Kat's bent head. Her braided hair flashed black and blue in the chinks of light. She was on the far side, disappearing through the deep stacks of pottery, moving pieces here and there.

"Don't spread this around," Merimose said. "It's not a secret, but we don't want people to panic. Basically, a servant was attacked in Khonsu Street and almost killed. He was found unconscious, his head bleeding."

"Right in the middle of all those glittering mansions?"

Merimose nodded. "We patrol the area regularly. You can imagine how upset people are. Unfortunately, my men on duty that morning saw nothing."

Kat worked her way closer, cleaning and arranging. The clonk of dishes being shuffled around broke the stillness of the air.

"Why was the servant attacked?"

"Well, he was carrying a scarab amulet. How the attacker knew that is anyone's guess. Apparently the thing was made of solid gold and studded with rare precious jewels—rubies, emeralds, you name it."

"What was a servant doing with an expensive scarab amulet?"

"The jewelry had been sent out some weeks ago to be cleaned and repaired. The household received a letter saying the amulet was ready for pick up. So the servant went to pick it up, and was bringing it home."

Zet's skin prickled, and he was suddenly on alert. "From where? I mean, where was the amulet cleaned?"

"At a place called the Kemet Workshop."

Kat's head snapped up and she gasped.

CHAPTER 21
THE MISSING AMULET

"Someone was attacked leaving the Kemet Workshop?" Kat asked, eyes wide.

"You have good ears," Merimose said.

Kat colored. Obviously, she'd been listening in the whole time.

Merimose said, "Apparently the Kemet Workshop has the best jewelers in Thebes. But it sounds to me like you've already heard of the place."

Zet and Kat glanced at one another.

"We have heard of it," Zet said.

"Something you want to tell me?" Merimose said, studying them both.

"I was there, yesterday," Zet said.

If the medjay was shocked or impressed, he hid it well. "Why?"

At that moment, a woman emerged from a dark alley and headed toward them. Clouds of perfume billowed around her as she approached. Kat's shoulders went around her ears.

"It's one of the women," she said in a tense voice. "I better go talk to her."

"Do you want my help?" Zet said.

"I can do it."

He nodded. "Tell her about mother going down river."

"I hope she tracked the missing orders down," Kat said.

"So do I." He desperately wanted the stall back to normal, with happy customers, and without the worry they'd be kicked out of the market and lose their business.

Merimose didn't pry.

"Thanks for giving me a few minutes with your brother," the medjay said. Then he followed Zet out of the hot sunlight, back to the shaded, private area at the rear of the stall.

Zet offered his uniformed friend a cushion.

"Ah, that feels good. I've been on my feet since before dawn," Merimose said. "So what were you doing at the workshop?"

"My best friend, Hui, took a position there as apprentice."

Zet told him about his run-in with Snaggletooth when he first tried to visit Hui. He went on to explain how he'd convinced Delilah to attend the semi-annual visit.

"So you got inside?"

"Not easily, but yes," Zet said.

"And what were your thoughts on the place? I know you've got a sharp pair of eyes."

"I thought it was creepy. There are spying slots everywhere. And they searched us on the way out. And everyone seemed to be acting really strange. Including my friend, Hui. And the owner was weird."

Merimose nodded, thoughtful. "We did notice the slots. I don't have a problem with them. Probably a good security measure. As for the rest, they're no doubt on guard given what's going on."

"Then you don't think it's suspicious?"

"In what way?" Merimose said.

"Maybe someone from the shop stole the jewels. They knew the servant had them."

"Unlikely," Merimose said. "Why would they do that? The place exudes wealth. Even if the piece were worth a lot, it wouldn't be worth risking the shop over. In fact, it would be bad business. Not only that, it's too obvious. It would just point right back to them if they stole a piece every time it left the workshop."

Zet nodded, thoughtful. "But was it worth a lot? Like a giant fortune?"

"It was worth a lot. But like I said, not enough to steal."

"Maybe they're in trouble? Maybe they need the money?"

"No. They're fully paid up with their creditors. In fact, Kemet pays early, I'm told. And if his servants' clothing is anything to go by, Kemet's rolling in wealth. That can't be it. He has a solid business going. I'm told he makes pieces for Pharaoh's wife and daughters. Maybe even some of the royal jewels."

"Humph." Zet scraped at the ground with his foot. "Did you at least search the place for it?"

Merimose grinned with that bright, flashing smile. "That's why I like you. We think alike. Yes, I searched for it. Of course, I searched for it. I don't care how things look, or how wealthy he is." His smile faded a little. "But no luck. It's not there. We tore the place apart."

Zet pictured the servant who'd searched his bag, and decided they'd gotten a taste of their own medicine. He smiled. "I bet they didn't like that."

"No, to put it mildly. We searched Kemet's residence as well."

"He doesn't live there?"

Merimose shook his shaved head. "Nope. Kemet's got a great mansion on the river. You've probably seen the place on your way to your friend Padus's papyrus plantation. It's the second to last house on the way out of town."

Zet stared off for a moment, imagining the road. "I think I know the one."

"The place is practically a palace. Statues leering down from every corner. Pillared hallways and courtyards. He welcomed me and my men in like a lord, and sat back drinking wine while we turned the place upside-down. That's what convinced me."

"Of what? His innocence?"

Merimose rubbed his neck. "Yep. I almost wanted him to be guilty. Smiling little beetle he is. Not my sort. But justice is justice, and I don't have to like all our citizens. I just have to protect them."

Through a gap in the curtained back area, Zet saw that the special orders woman had left. Kat was helping another customer, who'd chosen several dishes. Kat pulled an armful of reeds from a sack and stacked layers of them between the dishes. The dry plants crunched and crackled; their dry, fragrant scent filled the air.

"There's something else I need to tell you," Zet said.

"Oh?"

Zet itched his neck. He wasn't sure what Merimose thought about trespassing, but the man needed to know. "We snuck in there last night. I talked to my friend, and he pretty much told me something was going on."

The man's dark eyes sparked with interest. "What's going on, then?"

"Well—that's the thing. He couldn't tell me much, because guards showed up."

"Oh."

"I did learn one thing, though, he says Kemet's partner was gotten rid of somehow, because he'd made a big mistake."

"Gotten rid of? I don't like the sound of that."

"Not only that, Hui said Kemet's planning a shipment on the first day of the festival. And he said if we searched them, we could catch them."

"A search is not possible. Not without just cause. Kemet has proven himself innocent, we searched him completely. I'd need solid proof to do it again."

"But you have to!"

"Did Hui say what was in the shipment?"

"No, but does it matter?"

"Yes. As far as what you've told me, Kemet's done nothing wrong. He's bound to make shipments, it's a business after all. And if it eases your worries, my men are examining every ship before it leaves Thebes. They're looking for stolen scarabs, and any illegal shipment will be found, no matter what it is."

"But what about Kemet's partner disappearing?"

"Most likely apprentice gossip. People make up rumors. Especially when they're cooped up with each other for a long time. Look, like I said, I'm not a fan of Kemet. But he's wealthy. I don't think he'd sabotage his business over a few baubles."

What more could Zet say?

Still, he was sure Hui was in danger. Hui said so himself.

Merimose stood. "I need to get back to my office. As for you, just focus on your stall here. It's a good one."

CHAPTER 22
CRACKED

Merimose was nearly out of the square, when Zet had a sudden brain flash.

"Merimose!" Zet shouted. He sprinted past the goat pen, and a stall selling cabbages and carrots. "Merimose, wait up!"

Merimose stopped at a pen of honking geese. He raised one brow, waiting.

Shoppers watched as if wondering what business a twelve-year-old, barefoot nobody could have with the head medjay. Merimose did look impressive, with his polished sword and breastplate gleaming in the sunlight. If you didn't know him, he might even frighten you. Zet realized then just how lucky he was to call such an important man his friend.

"Well?" Merimose asked.

"I had a question."

"I told you to stay out of this one," Merimose warned.

"I know. I was just wondering—" He blurted out, "You know the servant who was attacked? Whose house did he work at? You never said."

Merimose's face darkened. "And I don't plan to. Stay out of it, Zet.

Don't you dare go questioning people in the Khonsu District. That servant was almost killed. These are dangerous people."

"But I helped you before, on another case. Maybe I can help now."

"You lucked out last time."

"Ouch," Zet said, stung. "It was a bit more than luck."

"This isn't a game. People could die."

Zet shuffled his feet. Yes, people could die, maybe even Hui. But Merimose didn't seem to understand that. Zet glanced down at the honking geese. The closest bird ruffled its feathers and blinked hopefully. Zet wished he had a handful of grains.

How could he convince Merimose that Hui needed help?

Merimose cut in on his thoughts. "I need to get back to my office. If you hear from your friend, report it to me. Understood?"

Zet nodded.

Merimose studied him, his face suspicious. "I'm serious, Zet, this case is too dangerous for you to go meddling around."

"Zet," Kat called, saving him from answering. "I need you!"

"Gotta go," Zet said, glad to escape.

The mid-morning swarm had descended. Things got busy, and it wasn't until closing time that Zet remembered the ivory ball. When they'd finished packing up for the evening, he stuck it under his arm.

"Come on, let's go home, I'd rather look at it there," he told Kat.

They ran, headlong through the streets, enjoying the cool air and the shadowed paving stones against their bare feet.

Suddenly, a man stepped out of his doorway and slammed into Zet.

The linen-wrapped ball flew one way, Zet the other. Eyes on the flying package, Zet somersaulted and stretched as far as he could. The ball landed in his fingertips. But his relief was short lived. The man lost his footing. He took Zet and the ball down with him.

They landed in a heap.

The ball made a sickening crunch.

"Watch where you're going," the man grumbled.

"Sorry," Zet said. Gingerly, he lifted his package into his arms. Even without unwrapping it, he knew the ball was broken.

The man's face softened. "I hope it wasn't something important."

"It wasn't your fault," Zet said. "I'm sorry I knocked you down."

After that, Zet and Kat walked more slowly. Their route took them down a busy thoroughfare. People bumped up against Zet in their hurry to get home. With each jolt to the package, he could feel a loose piece of ivory moving around.

"Stop," Zet told Kat. "Let's go back there behind the temple of Maat. I want to see how badly it's broken."

She nodded and they padded quietly past the towering structure.

The sky was still blue, despite the late hour. A pointed obelisk stood in the distance, framed between the walls of the narrow alley. Hieroglyphs had been carved into the stone; the writing stretched up as far as he could see.

"Okay, Hui," he said. "This ball of yours better tell us something."

He removed the linen, and dropped the covering to the ground.

The globe was still in one piece. A crack, however, zigzagged across its milky surface. Zet pried the crack apart. It was hard to see inside, but there was definitely something in there. Something pale brown. It almost looked like . . . no, that couldn't be right.

"Here goes nothing." Crouching, he smashed the ball against the flagstones.

The crack widened.

"Zet!" Kat gasped, her voice a mixture of horror and curiosity.

"Hui said to look at it. Well, I'm looking at it." He smashed it again. This time, the ivory came apart in two jagged pieces. His mouth dropped wide when he saw what the ball contained. He'd been right.

Kat's brow creased. "Is that bread?"

"Yep."

"Is that for padding or something? Do they normally put bread in ivory carvings?"

Zet rolled his eyes.

"No," she said, coloring. "No, I guess that would be stupid. It must be a clue then."

Zet pondered the roll. One half of the ivory shell still clung to it.

"Did you talk about bread when you were there?" Kat asked.

"Not really. Well, I guess sort of. At lunch, we had bread from the bakery next door. It was good, and we talked about it being good. That's about it."

"Maybe he wants you to talk to the people at the bakery?" Kat said.

"But he could have just said so on the roof." Zet pried the remaining ivory shell from it, set the shell down and turned the bread roll over. "There's a hole in the bottom."

"Let's see!"

Zet wedged a finger into the crust. "I think there's something in there. Yes, I feel something."

"What is it?"

"Something metal."

"Pull it out!"

Zet ripped the bread in half. A gleaming object fell into his lap. He gasped.

"A golden scarab," Kat breathed.

CHAPTER 23
A SCARAB OF GOLD

Zet stared at the object in his hand, unable to believe his eyes. The scarab had to be worth a fortune. Its jewels winked at him, and the polished gold seemed to give off a light of its own. A large red stone had been set in the middle, and the beetle itself was colored with crushed blue lapis.

"Don't let anyone see," Kat hissed.

Zet snatched the linen cover and partially wrapped it again. "This thing is crazy," he said. "It's like something Pharaoh would have."

"I know. But Zet, it's a scarab! Which means it's all connected."

"Yes, but how?" Zet frowned, trying to put himself in Hui's shoes.

What was Hui trying to say? Zet turned the scarab over, shielding it from prying eyes with the linen. When he saw the underside, his confusion grew.

"What in the name of the gods? Look at this."

The scarab beetle's belly was not gold, or bejeweled in any way. Instead, it was a dusty red color.

The bottom is made of . . ." He picked at it with one fingernail. "Clay?"

"Clay?" Kat said. "Let me see that." She took it from him.

"That is the strangest thing I've ever seen," Zet said. "It's the most expensive thing in the world if you look at the top, and the cheapest bauble known to mankind if you look at the bottom." He ran a hand over his scalp and let out a frustrated groan. "Hui," he said, speaking to the sky. "This would be a lot easier if you hid a note in there."

"He can't write," Kat said.

"I know."

"And neither can you."

"Okay, okay. Don't rub it in. Little Miss I-learned-hieratic-script-and-you-should-have-too."

"Well maybe now you see why it was a good idea. What did you want him to do, dictate a rescue note to Kemet's scribe?"

Zet rolled his eyes.

"But hold on," she said. "Let me see it again." Kat crouched down, holding the underside to face the dying light. "There's something here, scratched on the bottom."

Zet bent closer. She was right.

Two lines, side-by-side, with a connecting line at the bottom.

"It's the symbol for the number two," he said.

She nodded. "It must mean something. They're carefully drawn. It's obvious he put the symbol there for a reason."

But what reason?

Hui had done the best he could do by making this missive. It must have been dangerous; he would have had to make it in secret. But what was Hui trying to say? What did a strange, half gold, half clay scarab, with the number two on the bottom, embedded in a piece of bread mean? How was it connected to the scarab thefts? Or the shipment? Or Kemet's missing partner?

Feeling more frustrated than ever, they headed home. Once inside, Zet bee-lined for the kitchen and hid the scarab at the bottom of a basket of onions.

"No one will look for it here," he said.

"What are we going to do?" Kat asked.

"Tomorrow I'll go talk to the people at the bakery," he said.

Kat nodded. "They must know something." She let out a sigh of relief. "Maybe we don't know what the amulet means, but I feel like we're getting somewhere. I really do. And you know what, there's something else to look forward to."

"What's that?"

"Finally we're going to have an answer for those women. Mother comes home tomorrow."

"You're right. Thank the gods for that!"

With this cheerful thought, the two of them rummaged around the kitchen and put together a simple meal.

Kat carried bowls of food to the dining area; Zet set two lamps flickering on the table to chase away the darkness. They munched on thick slices of bread, heaps of spicy, chickpea stew, and garlicky, roasted vegetables. There was a jug of good, cold fermented barley water to wash it down. And for dessert, there was a pale yellow sweet cake. It was so delicious that they ate nearly half of it, drizzling their thick pieces with honey.

Finally, satisfied, Zet groaned and leaned back against the wall.

"What's that you're wearing around your neck?" Zet asked her.

Kat's hands went to it. "My pendant Hui made," she said in a high voice.

"Yeah, but beside it. The other thing on the chain."

She shrugged.

"Is that a protection amulet?" he said, squinting at the tiny roll of papyrus.

"Don't laugh."

"Am I laughing?"

"Yes."

"Please don't tell me you got that from Akar."

Kat colored.

"It's not demons. I'm telling you, it's something else. We have a scarab here from Hui. Obviously this whole thing has something to do with the workshop."

"Maybe," she squeaked. "Or maybe the demons will come here looking for that scarab, and we'll really be in trouble."

Zet tried hard not to laugh. He really did.

But he couldn't help it. Somehow, the thought of demons rushing in the door and searching the onion basket made him laugh until tears streamed down his face.

Kat punched his arm, but she was grinning. "Just help me clear the dishes, big brother."

CHAPTER 24
A CONTEST

On the way to work the next morning, Zet was thoughtful.

"I just wish there was some way to question the people in Khonsu Street," he said.

"You mean to ask for information about the attack on the servant?" Kat said.

"Yes. Even if it's not the right house, people gossip, everyone over there must know about it. Maybe I could learn something useful. But it's not like I could just go knock on someone's door and say, 'Hi, I'm Zet. Would you tell me what you know about the servant who was attacked? And by the way, has anyone stolen your scarabs?'"

Kat giggled. "No. Probably not."

"Anyway, maybe I'll learn something from the bakers. You're sure you don't mind if I go over there after we open up?"

"I can manage the stall," she said. "We have to help Hui. We don't have a choice."

Kat chewed her lower lip as she walked. He knew that look. She was smart, even though he'd never actually tell her that, and she was onto something.

"What are you thinking?" Zet said.

"It's a long shot."

"What is?"

"We could have a contest."

Zet stared at her, completely baffled. This was the last thing he expected her to say. "A contest?"

She outlined her plan. "It might work, right?"

His heart leapt. "It's good. It's really good."

As Zet opened up, Kat disappeared into the back of the stall.

"How's it going?" he called. "Are you almost finished?"

"Almost."

He wandered back and found her kneeling on the ground, writing on a big piece of linen.

"There," she said, with a final flourish of her brush. She held it up. "What do you think? It says: Happy Opet Festival. Enter to win this bowl."

"It's perfect," Zet said.

"And this is the bowl." She held up a big, brightly colored serving bowl that was certain to stand out. Painted blue ibis birds flew gracefully around its rim.

"Don't forget to get their street addresses," Zet said.

"Like I would. I'm not stupid. In case you forgot, this was my idea." She went out front to hang up her sign. "Help me with this, and then go to the bakery."

Zet helped her hang the sign, but decided to hang around in the hopes they'd get lucky early. Dusty light filled the stone plaza. At the stall next door, Geb, the old herb-vendor, removed the lids from his wares and set them out on display. The scent of cardamom, cinnamon and cumin rose from the mounds of brightly colored spices. Across the way, Salatis piled fresh golden dates into his baskets.

Customers were flooding in, too. The jar of entries started filling up fast.

Everyone wanted a chance at winning the beautiful bowl.

"Anyone from the Khonsu Street area?" Zet asked, for the tenth time.

"Stop asking me!" Kat said. "Just go to the bakery, will you? You're driving me crazy."

"All right, all right," he said, grinning.

"But Zet?" she said, looking suddenly worried.

"Yeah?"

"Promise you won't let the Kemet workshop people see you in there."

He hadn't thought of that. What if one of the men from next door came to the bakery to buy bread? They'd recognize him as Hui's friend from visiting day. And then they might connect him with the distur-bance from the night before. How would he explain his presence in the artisan quarter? It could be bad. Very bad.

Still, to Kat he said, "They wouldn't remember me. I'm just another kid."

"Okay," she said doubtfully.

With that, Zet took off at a run.

Hopefully he could get in and out, questions answered, without being seen by Kemet's henchmen.

CHAPTER 25
INTO THE OVEN

Zet wound his way back to the artisan quarter. The route was beginning to feel familiar, and he made his way quickly through the streets. He passed the familiar stench of the tannery, covering his nose as he ran.

How could anyone spend his days working there?

But that was not his problem. Right now, he had bigger things to worry about. The block with the bakery and the Kemet workshop was right around the corner. As he neared, he hoped to lose himself in the crowds. But unlike near his market square, crowds in this part of Thebes were thin. If he'd been clever, he might have thought to disguise himself. Hui would have; that's for certain. He'd have pulled out his mother's face paints, like some black kohl, to draw a crazy beard on his face or something.

Too late now.

Zet reached the familiar block and paused in the shadow of a doorway to survey the scene. To his relief, the locked gate was deserted. Not that Kemet would bother posting a guard. His henchmen wouldn't be expecting Zet to return. Especially in broad daylight. Only someone stupid would do that.

Right?

But Zet wasn't stupid. He was just determined to save his best friend.

He took a step out of the shadows when the barbed gate to the Kemet workshop slammed open. Zet ducked back. Snaggletooth and an equally large thug stepped out.

Frantic that he'd been seen, Zet tried the door handle behind him. It turned, and he opened the door a fraction and slipped inside. Heart thumping, he waited, expecting Snaggletooth to barge in and strangle him.

A moment passed. He risked a peek and saw Snaggletooth and the other man pass by. Zet sagged against the door in relief. He glanced around the room he was in. There were shelves full of what appeared to be woven sandal soles. A table held tools, and half a dozen sandals midway through construction.

He heard the sound of someone whistling in the adjoining room.

With a quick glance to make sure the coast was clear, Zet hurried back out into the street.

A moment later, he was standing in the warm front room of the bakery. The most delicious scents filled the air. Cinnamon and dates and the yeasty smell of rising dough.

The reception room was really just a small cubicle with a counter down the middle. Behind the counter, a rack with various breads on display rose to the ceiling. Next to the rack, a curtained doorway led to an area beyond.

On the counter sat a little bell. It was beautifully made, and he wondered if they'd got it from the Kemet workshop next door.

Zet picked it up and rang it.

A moment later, a woman thrust the curtain aside and stepped out. She was stooped and wrinkled, her skin dark from the sun. A puckered scar ruined whatever beauty she may have once had.

Before the curtain closed, Zet caught a glimpse of the baking courtyard beyond. The roof was open to the sky and on the ground were several pits loaded with hot coals. He'd seen bread being baked before, and knew bakers did it by placing lidded clay pots full of dough directly into the coals. He sold bread-baking pots himself. He wondered if they used his pots here.

"Can I help you?" the scarred woman said in a warbling voice.

"Yes. At least I hope so."

She wiped her hands on a spotless towel that hung from her waist. "What can I get you? A bread round, like this? Or something sweet perhaps?"

Zet fumbled in a small pouch. He'd brought a few deben to barter for bread, sure that he'd get better information if he bought something. "Two sweet rolls, please."

She smiled and fetched two plump buns from a basket. Zet handed over the deben, and she gave him several copper kite in return.

"I was wondering if I could ask you some questions?" Zet said.

At this, she stiffened. "What sort of questions?"

"About the workshop, next door. The Kemet Workshop?"

Her face hardened. "I don't have time."

"It would only take a minute. I have a friend over there. He's an apprentice, and I'm worried that—"

The curtain was thrust aside, and a second woman stepped out. She had no disfiguring scar, but apart from that, she looked identical to the first. Zet realized they were twins.

"What do you want, boy?" the second woman asked. "What's going on, Kissa?"

"Nothing," said Kissa, shooting Zet a warning glance. "He's just leaving. Aren't you, young man."

"No. Wait, listen, please! I think my friend wanted me to talk to you. He gave me some bread and . . ." Some sense of caution made him stop talking. Maybe this wasn't what Hui wanted him to do.

Kissa had her hands around the towel, and her knuckles were white with tension. "And what? He gave you some bread and what did he say?"

"Just—" He looked from one dark, wrinkled face to the other. Several months ago, he would have trusted these women without question. But he'd begun to learn that people weren't always what they seemed. Still, why had Hui sent him the bread to begin with?

The baker-twins were waiting.

"Just," Zet began, "My friend said I should ask you if you have a message for me."

"A message? Why would we have a message?" Kissa said, her hand going to her old scar.

"We wouldn't," snapped her sister. "We don't carry messages. If he had a message, he should have told you himself." Her voice had risen, and her eyes flashed.

"You have your bread," said Kissa in a gentler tone. She glanced out the door, and back at Zet again. "Now quick. Go."

"Maybe we shouldn't let him."

"Don't be a fool, Kakra," Kissa said. "I smell bread burning. Please, go back inside."

Kakra looked furious, but the fear of burned bread won out. She left.

Turning to Zet, Kissa said, "Now go, run, and keep away. Understand?"

"No, I don't," Zet said.

She was trembling. "We don't like nosy children. Please don't make me force you to leave."

CHAPTER 26
HOME SILENT HOME

Zet was more confused that ever as he headed back to his market stall. He hurried there, almost in a daze, barely noticing the people around him. Crowds bumped him this way and that. All he could think about was getting back to Kat and telling her about the strange reactions of the women.

What could have made them act that way? Were they afraid of Kemet? Had something happened to put them on guard? Had they, perhaps, witnessed the murders somehow, and now they were terrified to speak in case Kemet set his henchmen on them? Finally, he reached the square. He saw Kat up ahead, haggling with a pair of men over a large clay urn, used to store wine.

Zet waited until the men left, and then told her all about the strange sisters.

She looked completely baffled. "That is so strange. I was sure Hui wanted you to go there. What else could the bread mean?"

"I have no idea." Zet handed over a sweet bun. They munched in silence.

The bakery had been a dead end.

Their only lead now was Khonsu Street. He desperately hoped they'd find a winner for the bowl soon. They were running out of time.

The festival was in two days!

That left only tomorrow. Because the following day, the shipment had to be stopped. According to Hui, it was the only way to help him escape alive.

Until Zet could figure out a better plan, there was nothing left but to focus on work. He moved about, polishing plates and vases. He helped customers sort through all the beautiful choices to find just the right thing. He wrapped packages, and did his best to smile and say all the right things. Kat was also going through the motions, but it was clear that her mind, like his, was elsewhere.

The day inched forward. No one from Khonsu Street entered to win the bowl. Zet and Kat headed home in silence.

The thought of seeing his mother and baby brother, however, lifted his mood somewhat. Zet could hardly wait to see them.

When they reached their street, however, Zet frowned.

The windows were dark.

He ran up the steps and pushed open the door.

"Hello?" he called.

Nothing.

Kat wrapped her arms around herself. "Where are they?"

"I don't know! She should have been back, hours ago."

Kat looked frightened.

"I'm going to the boat dock," Zet said.

"I'm coming with you."

But when they reached the boat dock, it was deserted. Finally, they found a familiar looking man who'd helped them unload goods in the past.

"Nope," the man said, "I haven't seen your mother. Or the potters' boat for that matter. I've been here all day. Now don't look so worried, children," he added. "She probably just got held up. She'll be here tomorrow. Go on home and have your dinner."

They wandered away from the man.

The river lapped gently against the water's edge. The night air felt humid and heavy, pressing down, making it hard to breathe.

"I'm sure she's fine," Kat burst out, but didn't sound sure.

"You're right," Zet said. "I'm sure she is."

Three men sat in a circle of lamplight, two of them playing a game of Senet. One started to shout that the other was cheating. The other man leapt up, balling his fists. Kat watched in horror as they shouted at each other, and Zet was sure they were going to start a fistfight.

"Let's get out of here," he said. He walked quickly, his own anger bubbling up. Nothing in his life was working right. He felt trapped. He had to do something. He turned to Kat. "I'm going to Kemet's mansion to look around."

"When?" Kat asked. This time, she didn't say she wanted to come along. She didn't argue that it was dangerous, either. Clearly, she knew they were running out of choices as well as he did.

"I'm going tonight. I'll walk you home first."

"I can walk home by myself," she said.

And so, Zet set off at a run for the edge of town.

Kemet's mansion was just as Merimose had described it. Huge and looming, and surrounded by high, white walls. A pair of towering statues presided over the front entry, with bodies of giants and faces molded to look like Kemet himself. Music drifted from somewhere inside, along with the burble of chatter and laughter.

It sounded like Kemet was hosting a large dinner party.

This could be good. It could provide the cover Zet needed.

He searched the wall for a spot to climb in. A cluster of date palms towered over the rear of the complex, leaned up against the walls. He made it quickly up the trunks, and dropped down onto the manicured grounds on the other side.

A dog snarled.

Zet's head snapped up. Three large hounds crouched at the open door to the house. The snarling dog bared its teeth. Then it shot toward Zet, barking. In a flash of fur, the other two dogs followed. They bore down on him in a flash of teeth and fur.

Zet turned and threw himself at the wall. There were no toeholds. Frantic, he made for a birdbath, jumped onto it, and leapt for the top of the wall. He missed. The dogs were nearly on him. And men were shouting now, too. Desperate, he leapt onto the birdbath a second time.

Teeth caught hold of his ankle.

He felt skin tear.

He wrenched his leg free. Threw himself at the wall. His fingers latched onto the top of it. Holding on in a death grip, he pushed off with his toes and cartwheeled over. He landed on all fours.

Then he sprinted.

Fast.

The doors were opening, and the dogs were shooting out.

Zet found a palm grove near the river, climbed the nearest tree, and stayed there until the coast was clear.

CHAPTER 27
A WINNER!

A strange mood gripped the little market square the next morning.

Sales were up at Akar's stall; the line to buy magical devices wound out and down one of the side alleys. Some people were terrified of the demon army.

Others, in contrast, spoke in excited voices about the Opet Festival opening ceremonies on the following day. There was to be a chariot race down the Avenue of the Sphinxes.

"I heard the Royal sons organized it," a man told Geb.

The herb-seller said, "I heard that, too. And I heard the sons will be racing, with Pharaoh, the Royal wife, and Pharaoh's royal mother in attendance."

Zet was listening to this discussion, but his mind was elsewhere. All he could think of was that the clock was ticking down. He only had today left. Tomorrow morning, the shipment would be leaving the Kemet workshop. And he was no closer to stopping it. Maybe he should talk to Merimose. And say what?

Suddenly, Kat jolted him back to the present.

"Zet," she gasped, grabbing his arm. Her face was alight. "We have a winner for the serving bowl!"

His heart seemed to stop. "You mean we have an entry from Khonsu Street?"

Kat nodded furiously, her cheeks red with excitement. "I told the woman you'd bring it to her house later today. She seemed happy, and she said that servants manned the house all day, and that they would accept the bowl for her if she hadn't returned."

He leaped into the air with a shout.

Geb and his customer turned in surprise.

"Er, just excited about the chariot race," Zet said.

He ran after Kat, who had disappeared into the back to wrap it.

"Don't bother, there's no time," he said, taking the bowl. "What's the address?"

Kat took out a scrap of old broken pottery, on which she'd written it down. "Okay. Her house is on the corner of Khonsu and Temple Way. The delivery entrance is a wooden double-door, with a brass knocker in the shape of a cow's head."

"I'm there," Zet said.

"You should try to beat her home," Kat said. "It'll be a lot easier to talk to her servants. I bet every servant in Khonsu Street has gossiped about it, since they're probably friends with the man who was attacked. I bet they know more than anyone."

Zet grinned. "I can't believe the contest worked! For once, little sister, you really used those smarts of yours."

"For once?" she cried.

"Gotta go," he said with a grin. Then he gave her braids a tug and took off with the bowl through the crowds for Khonsu Street.

The further Zet got from the market district, the quieter the streets became. Large walls hid expensive homes. Shade trees, heavy with fruits, hung over the wall tops. The scent of hidden flower gardens filled the air. Someone had swept the streets, and the stones felt smooth, hot and dry under Zet's bare feet.

He found his way to Temple Street, and followed it west a few blocks. The sound of voices carried to him from the distance. It sounded like a crowd had gathered, with many people talking at once. Several voices rose in excitement, and were lost in the chatter.

Zet turned into Khonsu Street and saw that it was full of people.

Gripping the bowl tightly in both arms, he slowed his walk and approached.

To his right, he spotted a pair of double doors with a knocker in the shape of a cow's head. Instead of stopping, however, he kept walking toward the crowd.

He could see several men dressed in medjay uniforms. One turned, as if sensing Zet's eyes on him. Zet saw it was his friend, Merimose.

Zet grinned, but the head medjay looked less than pleased to see him. The big man excused himself from the two men he was speaking with, and broke away from the crowd.

"What's going on?" Zet asked.

"A better question might be, what are you doing here?" Merimose said.

Zet indicated the bowl. "Bringing the winner their prize. We held a contest. Someone from Khonsu Street won it."

"Uh huh." Merimose looked skeptical. "Funny coincidence, someone winning the bowl from this area."

Zet rubbed his neck.

The big medjay crossed his arms over his polished chest-plate. "I don't suppose this contest has anything to do with you coming to investigate?"

"Why would you say that?" Zet asked, trying to look innocent.

"Zet, I told you to stay out of it. People have been attacked. It's not a game."

Zet shuffled his feet. He indicated the crowd. "Has someone else been mugged?"

With a snort, Merimose looked skyward. "Do you ever give up?"

"Look, the only reason I care is because I'm worried about my best friend. I'm sure you can understand that."

Sighing, Merimose met Zet's eyes. He nodded. "I can. But you're not a trained fighter. And these people are dangerous."

"So what happened? Why are all those people standing in the street?"

"A house was robbed."

"Oh."

"They stole a casket of jewels."

"Scarabs?"

"Must have been looking for them, that's my guess." Merimose glanced over his shoulder at the crowd. "I don't even know why I'm telling you this, but we found the casket abandoned on the next block over. Nothing was taken. It's all still in there."

Zet let out a frustrated breath. "I don't get it. Why do they only want scarabs?"

"That's the puzzle, isn't it?" Merimose said. "And since I know you're going to ask, the owner has never purchased services from the Kemet Workshop."

"Oh." Zet wondered if he should tell Merimose about the half clay, half golden scarab Hui had given him. But it wasn't proof of any kind.

"Merimose!" shouted a uniformed man. He looked hot and irritated, as did the two wealthy looking people standing with him.

"Be right there," Merimose called back. To Zet he said, "Deliver your bowl, but don't let me catch you hanging around. Got it?"

"Why would I hang around?"

Merimose gave him a dark look. "Really, my friend. I mean it."

"All right, all right," Zet said.

CHAPTER 28
KHONSU STREET

Delivering the bowl turned out to be harder than Zet had hoped. No one answered the door, despite his repeated banging. He was starting to grow worried, when a slim young girl detached from the crowd and approached at a fast walk.

She was dressed simply in a long, white dress, and her feet were bare. But she had the prettiest face Zet had ever seen.

"You are looking for someone?" she asked.

"The bowl. I mean, I'm bringing this bowl. To the house," Zet said. For some reason, his face was turning hot and he was having trouble getting his words out.

"I can take it," she said with a smirk.

"Who are you?" Zet asked, annoyed by her self-satisfied expression.

"I work here. That's who. And who are you?"

Zet drew himself up to his full height. "I own the stall that raffled this bowl off to the winner. And your owner won it. That's who."

If she was impressed, she didn't show it. "Then I shall give it to my owner. Hand it over." She held out her slender arms to receive it.

Zet stood there a moment, unsure why this pretty girl was so unsettling. Finally, still holding the bowl, he said, "Do you know anything about what's going on over there?"

"Of course," she scoffed. "Some box of jewelry was stolen, and the thief didn't like any of it, so they tossed it on the next street over."

"But the jewelry must have been worth something."

She shrugged her delicate shoulders. "I suppose so. Although I had a look just now and it was all terrible stuff. Big and clunky and really old-fashioned. Probably they realized they could never sell it."

"They could melt it down, though, couldn't they? And sell the gold?" Zet asked.

"I suppose. I hadn't thought of that."

"What's everyone saying about it over there?"

She laughed. "That it's the work of the demon army. That they were looking for scarabs to eat, and didn't find any. You should see some of them, I swear, they're terrified out of their minds. *We're all cursed!* You know, that sort of gibberish."

"And you don't believe it?"

She considered this a moment. "If you want my honest opinion, no. If a demon army had bothered to come here, to this street, I think we'd know about it."

Zet didn't bother to ask how they'd know. Instead, he said, "Then what is going on?"

Her face took on a focused look, as if she were trying to see something, or maybe put it all together. "Here's what I think. It's not just any scarab the thief wants. He's looking for one scarab in specific. Obviously, he's desperate to get it. He's taking a lot of risks, coming back to Khonsu Street again and again."

It was an interesting idea.

"But could one piece of jewelry be that important to someone?" he said.

She frowned at him. "Look, I don't feel like standing here arguing with you. Are you going to give me the bowl or not?"

He handed it over, thinking it a shame such a pretty girl could have such a sharp temper. She cradled the bowl tightly, and her eyes seemed to soften as she studied the design along its rim.

"The water-birds are pretty," she said.

"Thanks. We get our things from a pottery guild down river."

"I know," she said without looking him. "That was my village, once. I'll take good care of it," she said, and disappeared inside.

Zet stared after her, surprised at this turn of events. But there was no time to wonder about the girl and what had brought her away from her family. The afternoon shadows were growing longer. He needed to get back to his stall.

He left the well-swept streets of the Khonsu district behind.

Still, her theory about the jewels was a good one. Could Kemet be looking for a specific piece of jewelry? Trying to get it back, maybe? How did it all tie together?

So many questions swirled in his mind that his head hurt.

By the time he spotted the familiar tented awnings of the market-place, the wooden slats of the goat pen, and the baskets of produce up ahead, he had a pounding headache.

CHAPTER 29
FAKES

Zet rubbed his face as he wound behind the stacks of pottery. A group of women stood chattering away to Kat, all of them laughing in the afternoon sunlight. It was hard to imagine Hui, trapped in the gloomy workshop with its big guards and spying slots when Ra, the sun god, stood brightly overhead.

Zet caught snatches of the women's conversation.

"What do you think the Royal Wife will be wearing?"

"Something glorious. Do you remember that gown she wore last year?"

"The one made of solid gold?"

"It wasn't solid gold. Don't be silly."

"It was. I heard it was constructed all out of gold beads, held together with gold thread."

"Well I just acquired a copy of the Royal Wife's wedding necklace to wear," said a tall woman, changing the subject. She had her hair all done up on top of her head.

At her words, something sparked in Zet's mind. The hairs stood up on his neck.

"A copy?" he asked, joining the woman.

"You got it today? Is it in your bag? Let's see," said another.

The tall woman's face brightened, clearly enjoying the fuss. "It's right here."

"Zet," Kat said, trying to pull him aside. He saw by the set of her shoulders that something was wrong, and that her smiles and chatter had been nothing more than forced politeness. She was worried.

Still, he said, "Just a minute. I want to see them."

"But Zet!"

"Hold on."

The woman unwrapped the necklace and held it to the light.

Zet had never paid much attention to jewelry before, but now he found himself examining the glittering beads.

"Pretty, isn't it?" she said.

"Do lots of jewelers make copies of things?" he asked, trying to sound more casual than he felt.

"Certainly. Not many can afford the real thing. It's still expensive, but the beads are wooden instead of solid gold. They're painted with real gold leaf."

A chill ran through him. "And the other beads? The clear ones? They must be real."

"Some are colored glass, some are semi-precious stones that look similar to their more expensive cousins."

"You'd never guess," Zet said.

Is that what Hui was trying say with his scarab? That some of the jewels made at the Kemet workshop were fakes? Still, if lots of jewelers did it, then the fact Kemet's jewels were fake shouldn't be a problem.

As long as he told the truth.

What if he lied to people? Was it possible to make copies of jewels so well that people couldn't tell the difference?

If a person was skilled enough, Zet bet they could.

"Zet, you've seen it. Now can I please talk to you?" Kat whispered. Louder, she apologized to the woman for dragging her brother away.

When they reached the back of the stall her smile faltered. She was shaking all over.

"What's the matter?" Zet said quickly.

"Men came here," she gasped.

"What kind of men?"

"Horrible looking men. Like the ones from the workshop. I think it was the same people who chased us."

His heart slammed in his ears. "What did you do?"

Her face was pale. "Nothing. Fortunately, it was crowded. They asked for you, though. By name."

Zet swallowed. "I told Kemet I owned a pottery stall."

"Oh, Zet, It's all my fault! You know what this means, don't you? They've put it all together—the fact that Hui was out of his room, and me screaming in the garbage pit. They know it's connected."

"Well by that reasoning, it's my fault for going to see Hui in the first place. Forget it, okay? We're not going to get anywhere by blaming ourselves. So we made mistakes. We both did. We have to get Hui out. That's all."

"That's not all! The men will probably come back here."

"What did you say to them?"

"I told them I'd never heard of you," she said.

"Well, at least there's that." He grinned. "Most of the time, you probably wish it was true."

"Stop joking," she said, but still a whisper of a smile touched her lips.

The women had dispersed, and the crowds were beginning to thin.

"We should go home," Zet said. "There's no point in risking staying here any longer."

"I agree. But you should leave right now," Kat said, "Before they come back. I'll close up myself and meet you at home."

Zet decided not to argue. It was a good idea to distance himself from the stall. No point in getting them both in trouble.

"But I'm not going home until you're in the clear. I'll make myself scarce, but I'll keep an eye on you from a distance. I don't want them coming back and trying to drag you away for questioning."

The color drained from her face. "I hadn't thought of that."

Zet went to the back of the stall where he'd hid the scarab. It occurred to him then that if the thugs had managed to search the stall, and had found this piece, it would point straight to Hui.

He wrapped the scarab and snuck out the back, into the adjoining stall.

CHAPTER 30
FRIENDS

Geb, the grizzled herb-seller, glanced up and shot him a look. His white brows were thick and tufted; he looked like a serious, old bird. He was covering up his baskets of spices, herbs, clothing dyes and pounded wheat grain.

"Happy Opet Festival," Zet said.

Geb nodded. "And to you and your family."

Zet hurried into the nearest alley. It was deserted and dark in shadow. He looked both ways, and then scaled the wall. On the roof, he lay belly down and inched forward until he could see Kat far below across the square.

So far, so good.

She lifted stacks of plates and piled them against the rear of the stall. She dragged the big vase backward. She took out the thick sheets and tied them down. Geb said something to her. Kat replied with a smile.

Hurry up, Zet thought, and glanced toward one of the streets that led into the little square. His body went rigid. Two large, powerful looking men appeared.

Snaggletooth! And his henchman.

Zet looked back at Kat, unable to breath as he willed her to hurry up. She was still talking to Geb. What could be so important? He wanted to shout a warning, but that would draw the thugs' attention. His fists clenched, and sweat prickled on his neck.

Go! *Hurry up.*

Finally, she started to move off.

Across the square, the thugs were drawing closer. Kat kept moving, ducking through a stall hung with scarves, and then heading around the goat pen. The thugs had reached the stall. They looked this way and that.

Kat, however, had reached the entrance to an alley that would take her into the maze of streets. Zet allowed himself a small breath of relief. They weren't out of the clear yet. The thugs started to poke around their closed stall.

Then, to Zet's shock, Salatis, the grumpy date-seller, yelled, "Get away from there."

Snaggletooth turned and glared at the wiry, sun-wrinkled man.

"You heard me," Salatis crowed.

Geb joined in. "Move off. That stall's closed."

Zet could hardly believe it. Zet thought the two vendors wanted him kicked out. And there they were defending his wares? He wanted to cheer the pair of brave old men on. Snaggletooth marched at them with a menacing look, however, and Zet grew worried.

The thug could snap Salatis and Geb in half singlehanded.

"Move off, I say," came a third voice, speaking in a slow, spooky tone. It was Akar, the strange new vendor. He was waving some kind of wand. "Move off, I tell you!" he chanted, waving at Snaggletooth. "Be gone, big man."

Snaggletooth looked momentarily surprised. "What's it to you?"

"I shall curse you with horrible boils. Be gone!"

Zet didn't know whether to laugh or whoop with joy at the sight.

"What Akar here is trying to say," Salatis explained, "Is we protect our own."

"Really?" Snaggletooth said.

"Really." Salatis crossed his arms, his skinny legs planted like wishbones.

"And how are you going to do that, stork-legs?"

"This is how," came a fourth voice. The soft-spoken woman sold scarves. She stepped forward with a dozen other stall owners.

Then the rest appeared. They came out from under their awnings, one after the other. Skinny, fat, young and old.

Zet's heart swelled. He blinked back a few embarrassed tears.

Snaggletooth could never fight them all.

Zet had never felt so honored, so proud to be called a member of that group.

Snaggletooth swore under his breath. Clearly, he realized he'd been beaten. Without another word, the pair of scary men walked away. Just before Snaggletooth exited the square, however, he glanced around.

Zet ducked low against the roof. But he caught the look on the man's ugly face. Snaggletooth wore an expression so murderous, the hair stood up on Zet's arms.

If Zet wanted to stay among the living, he'd have to make sure they never crossed paths again. But that wasn't going to be easy. Not if he wanted to help Hui.

When the coast was clear, he slid to the ground and sprinted for home.

Kat met him at the door, her face a mask of fright.

"Mother's not back," she said.

The words hit him like a stone. He turned and ran for the wharf.

Kat pounded along behind, matching his strides.

At the wharf, they found the man they'd met the night before.

"Nope, still haven't seen her," he said. This time there was worry in his voice, too. Still, he added, "Now children, I'm sure there's a good reason."

"I want to hire a boat," Zet said. "Right now."

"Not possible. Do you see any boats here? They're all rented out for the festival ceremonies tomorrow. People hired 'em out so they could watch the chariot race along the Avenue of the Sphinx from the comfort of a boat. Can't say I blame 'em. There's going to be a lot of pushing and shoving to get good seats along the Avenue."

Zet was too dazed to answer.

Had something awful happened to their mother and Apu?

He and Kat stumbled home.

CHAPTER 31
UNDERSTANDING

Back home, Zet went straight to the household shrine. He knelt in front of the statue of Bastet. The cat goddess regarded him with her gold-rimmed eyes. He lit a cone of incense for her and stroked her smooth, ebony head.

"Please bring Mother and Apu home safe," he whispered. "And Hui, too."

Kat joined him, her face red and tearstained in the lamplight.

"What are we going to do?" she asked.

His stomach turned with fear. How could his mother be two whole days late? What if something happened? What if she never came back? The vision opened like a shadowy abyss. He hung on the edge of a future so black and horrible that he tore his mind away.

"I don't know, Kat," he said quietly.

They sat like that until the incense burned away to nothing.

Zet rubbed his face, and then looked at his little sister. "Maybe I can't help Mother right now. But I can still try to help Hui. I have to. There's no point in me sitting here any longer, it won't bring her home."

Kat wiped away her tears and blew her nose. "What are you going to do?"

"Remember those women talking about fake jewels?"

She nodded. "Kemet's making fakes and telling people they're real, isn't he. That's the meaning behind Hui's scarab."

"Yes. But I think it's more than that. There has to be a reason for the thefts. They don't fit into the puzzle. Why make fakes and sell them, and steal them back? I want to have another look at Hui's scarab."

In the kitchen, he pulled the package from its hiding place in the onion basket. He unwrapped it.

"What do you think this number two means?" he said. "Why did he put that there?"

Kat twisted her braid in her fist. "You know when we get pottery pieces from the guild, and there's more than one in the same style?"

"Yes."

"Well, on the bottom, the artist marks the matching pieces with a number. One, two, three, and so on. It makes it easier for me to keep records. If five matching plates come in, I mark that down. Then, when we barter one, I cross it off my list and I know how many we have left."

"Okay," he said, wondering where she was going with this.

"What if he's trying to say there are two fake scarabs? Could that be possible?"

Zet froze. "That's it. That's exactly it!"

"It is?"

"Yes! You're brilliant. Don't you see? There are two fake scarabs! Kemet got one of the fakes back when he attacked that servant in Khonsu Street last week. But there's still one more out there."

"What are you talking about? Why bother stealing something after he just sent it out the door?"

"Because he made a mistake."

Kat looked even more confused.

"Think about it—two scarabs went in for cleaning. Right? And maybe, instead of cleaning them, Kemet made two copies to send back, so he could keep the good ones for himself."

"Yes . . ."

"But when his partner made the two copies, he screwed them up. He switched the stones around by mistake!"

"You mean, like he gave one scarab a yellow stone for a head, and the other one got a blue head, when they were supposed to be the opposite?"

"Exactly. And any owner would spot the difference instantly."

"But how would Kemet know, if his partner's the one who made them?"

"The partner must have realized his mistake after. Maybe he picked up the real ones to put them away for safekeeping. And then it struck him the stones weren't right. And then he knew. So, he warned Kemet, who sent Snaggletooth after the servants. Except they only stopped one scarab from getting to its owner."

"Which means one scarab is still out there, like a ticking time bomb, waiting for the owner to look at it," Kat gasped.

Zet nodded. "I guess Kemet was mad enough that he got rid of the partner. Whatever that means." He shuddered. "And now he's forced Hui to do the man's dirty work. He's forced Hui into making his fakes."

The lamp guttered, casting creepy shadows dancing along the walls.

"That's where Hui was going in the boat that day," Kat said softly. "To the private workshop at Kemet's house. This is awful, Zet. I see why Hui said he can't escape. If Kemet had his partner killed, he'll kill Hui too for ratting him out." She held her stomach and groaned. "I feel sick."

"Well, I don't. I feel mad. The shipment must be all the real jewels. Kemet must ship them upriver to sell in another city. He's probably been doing it for years. No wonder he's so rich! But I'm going to bust him, and show everyone he's been replacing his repairs with fakes, and stealing the real things."

"Zet, if all this is true, then it's going to work out. Kemet will get caught eventually. The person with the mixed up scarab will take it out and look at it, and he'll raise the alarm. And the medjay will be brought in."

"I don't think Kemet plans to wait around."

"What do you mean?"

"My guess is he's going to escape, along with tomorrow's shipment, and disappear forever. The stolen gold and jewels will pay to keep him alive, wherever he goes. Even if he has to abandon his mansion and business here." Zet paced back and forth, running a hand over his scalp.

"You should go to the medjay. Right now," Kat said.

"And say what? They won't believe me, not without proof. I have to do it myself."

"How? Alone? You're just a kid!"

"I'll figure it out when I get there," Zet said.

CHAPTER 32
ACTION

In the kitchen, faint moonlight strobed through the straw roof overhead.

"I want to come—" Kat began.

"No." Zet's voice was flat. "Not after last time. Let me do this my way Kat. I don't want you screwing this up."

She looked upset, but said nothing.

Going to the stove, he took out some coals and blackened his face, arms, hands and feet. This time, he'd be going to the workshop in disguise. He needed every edge he could get. He smeared the coals around until he was dark and filthy.

Kat found a rough sack that once held emmer wheat grains. She cut holes for his neck and arms. "Wear this. Kemet's men will never recognize you dressed like a beggar."

He slid the rough outfit over his head. It was scratchy, and he knew he looked terrible. Which was great. She handed him a coil of twine. He wound it around his waist like a belt.

"It's a costume worthy of Hui," Kat said.

"It is, isn't it? He'd love it. No one's going to notice a filthy beggar like me now."

She wished him luck and he stepped into the night, wearing the biggest grin in the world. This was going to work.

He headed for the artisan quarter, but at the last moment, he switched directions. He'd give Merimose one last shot. Maybe the head medjay would believe him, if Zet told him the whole story. Stopping Kemet would be easy with a band of policemen to help.

He soon reached the police station.

The surrounding streets were deserted. Lamps flickered in sconces on either side of the station door. He hurried up the steps. Light spilled from the interior. The whitewashed office was like an oasis of bright safety in the dark night.

An officer stood just inside the front door.

"Whoa there, boy. Lost your way?"

"No, I'm looking for Merimose. The head medjay."

The big man look amused. "Are you now? Well, he's not here."

"I know I look strange," Zet said, "but, well, I'm in costume."

"Little late for a boy to be out in a party costume," said the big man.

The doorman's partner, who sat behind a desk, laughed. "That's your idea of a party costume?"

Zet recognized the deskman from earlier visits, but couldn't think of his name. "I wasn't at a party," Zet said. "I need help. I know who's behind the scarab thefts, and we have to stop them."

Both men looked sharply at him. "Stop who?"

"The people at the Kemet Workshop. They're planning a big shipment in the morning. You have to stop it."

Silence fell. A breeze crept through the front door, causing the lamps to flicker.

Zet shuffled his feet, waiting.

"What kind of shipment?" the deskman asked.

"Stolen jewels."

The officers shot him skeptic looks. Clearly, his appearance wasn't helping any. His sackcloth outfit was itchy beyond belief. He rubbed his belly, where the scratchiness was the worst. Both men watched, their mouths turning down at the corners.

"That's a story, if I've ever heard one," the doorman said.

"Boy," said the deskman, "If I was even inclined to believe you, which I'm not, no shipment leaves town without a search. Security has been stepped way up. And with the Royal Family out in full force tomorrow morning, every officer will be on duty."

Zet said, "But the thieves must know that. I'm sure they have a plan. Please—"

"Wait." The doorman grinned and stuck his head outside. "Someone's pulling a joke on us here, aren't they? I get it, Festival First Day station humor for us guys stuck here all night."

The deskman laughed. "Has to be Paneb. Was it Paneb?" he asked Zet. "An officer with an Eye of Horus tattoo on his right bicep? How much did he pay you?" He glanced outside too, as if expecting to see their friend laughing in the street.

"No one paid me," Zet said. "It's the truth."

"You're good," the deskman said. "Beggar-boy, I think you've got a career as an actor in your future."

"I'm not acting. Don't you recognize me? I helped Merimose before!"

"You're bringing the station chief into it? That's going too far." The doorman took Zet by his collar, lifted him with one burly arm and deposited him outside. "Joke's over."

"But it's not a joke. I'm telling you—"

"Clear out," the doorman said. He wasn't smiling.

Zet knew when to stop. He left before they decided to throw him in a cell overnight. He couldn't afford to get trapped behind bars.

Outside, a hush had fallen over the streets.

It was as if everyone were waiting with baited breath for what tomorrow would hold. The beginning of the Opus Festival, chariot race down the Avenue of the Sphinxes, and if the rumors were true, an attack from a demon army of dead Hyksos soldiers.

Zet knew now that the scarab-eating demons weren't real.

At least, he hoped so.

Something brushed his ankle. He leapt into the air with a yelp.

Yellow kitten-eyes gleamed at him in the velvet dark.

"You scared me," Zet whispered.

The ebony colored kitten reminded him of Bastet, their family goddess, back home. He breathed a sigh of relief. He bent and she let him scratch her ears.

Then she scampered off into a curtained doorway and was gone.

CHAPTER 33
BROKEN GOD

I f the Kemet Workshop had anything special going on, you couldn't tell from the street. Zet stared at the blackened iron gate, with its knife like bars sharpened to points at the top. No lamps were lit. Apart from the partial moon, the whole area was pitch black and silent.

Zet guessed he had four hours to wait until sunrise.

He decided to make use of his time by doing a full circuit of the workshop. He wanted to make sure the gated entry was the only exit through which the stolen shipment would come.

Halfway around, Zet reached the notorious, foul garbage pit.

Zet paused to peer through the wooden gate. His jaw dropped. Someone had cleaned the whole thing out. It was empty, from end to end. He thought of Kat screaming, sure there had been fingers grabbing her. But maybe there were other clues Kemet was worried might get found if the pit was examined.

He felt stupid for not thinking of it earlier.

But it was too late to worry about that now.

Still, Zet climbed over, wanting to get a closer look. The long, dark walls were stained with remains. A faint, foul odor still hung in the air.

He turned fully, looking in all directions, when something caught his eye.

Some kind of small statue leaned up against the gate.

Like it had been placed there on purpose.

Zet crouched down. A shudder of terror shot from the base of his neck to his ankles.

It was Hui's family god, Bes!

He'd recognize the cheerful statue Hui kept by his bedside anywhere.

The little dwarf god looked up at him with his happy face of stone. Except the dwarf wasn't quite himself. His right ear, which stuck out in a comical fashion, had been broken off. As had one of his legs. The sight of Bes so destroyed was like finding his best friend Hui, all smashed to pieces.

Was this a message? Was Kemet trying to say something, by leaving Hui's protective statue out here like this? Had he known Zet would return? Or worse, had Kemet just throwing Bes away because Hui was no longer . . .

Zet wouldn't finish the thought.

Hui was alive. He had to be. It couldn't be too late. It just couldn't!

In confused desperation, Zet searched for the little guy's arm. And then his ear. He held the god and his broken pieces to his chest, as if doing so could somehow keep his friend safe.

Zet's fear soon turned to fury.

He had to know if Hui was alive. He didn't care if what he was about to do was stupid. He was going in for a look.

"I'll come back for you," he told Bes.

Climbing onto the roof was harder this time, without the tall pile to climb over. Still, he found handholds in the rough walls, and hauled himself up. Taking less care than he should have, he dropped into the Kemet Workshop courtyard. On silent feet, he sprinted for Hui's room.

The door stood open. One boy slept on the bed to the left.

Zet's heart dropped to his toes.

Hui's bed was empty. Completely stripped to its frame. Not a shred of Hui's things remained. No clothing. No hippo's tooth.

Hui was gone.

In a daze, Zet backed out into the hall.

He heard voices heading his way. He wanted to run toward them. To shout at them, to demand what they'd done with his best friend. But what use would that be? None. He hated himself for leaving, but he had no choice.

He turned his back on Hui's empty bed and left.

Back in the garbage alley, Zet scooped Bes into his arms and clambered out. He cradled the broken god, as if it were his best friend himself. As if by keeping the god together, he could somehow bring Hui back.

He felt beaten down as he shuffled along the gritty street. The humidity made the air thick and hard to breathe. Partway along the block, someone had tried to grow a few potted plants. The stems, however, were straggly and dead. Zet pulled the pots out a little ways, and set Bes behind them. It was as good a hiding spot as any, and he couldn't carry the little god around if he wanted to confront Kemet and his shipment.

If nothing else, he'd confirmed there was only one way out of Kemet's workshop.

He found a dark alcove across the street and sank down to post up for the night.

If anything or anyone came out that door, he'd be on his feet in an instant.

It was time to end this nightmare.

CHAPTER 34
AND THEY'RE OFF

The mutter of voices made Zet start upright. He must have fallen asleep.

Dawn had begun to filter down into the humid, dusty murk. He cursed silently. All those big words to Kat about doing things himself—and here he'd fallen asleep?

Panic and a sickening feeling gripped him. What had he missed? How long had he been out? He rubbed his eyes hard and stared across the street.

Had someone come out the gate, while he dozed like a fool?

There was no way to tell.

Suddenly, the bakeshop's curtained doorway was thrust aside. A large wooden cart emerged into the street. Kissa, the kinder of the two twins—the one with the puckered scar—was pushing it.

Round loaves of bread had been piled high in the shape of a pyramid. The wheels creaked and groaned under the weight.

Kakra, the second twin, emerged. She took hold of the opposite side of the cart and helped push.

Zet ducked lower. Kissa and Kakra, however, didn't look around. Grim-faced, perhaps unhappy at having to work on a holiday, they trudged forward. Grit crunched under the turning wheels, and the cart took up a rhythm, rolling and grinding off down the street.

Zet let his head fall back against the wall behind him.

What should he do now?

Keep waiting?

He thought about the festival getting underway. Despite the early hour, the streets were probably already lined with people. Maybe he could find a medjay and report Hui missing. But there would be no pulling a man away now. Not with the events going on in town.

He was still pondering what to do when the gate to the workshop whispered open. Zet flattened himself against the wall.

Snaggletooth stepped out. The thug glanced over one muscled shoulder, into the workshop's dark alley entrance. He growled something. A second man replied, then emerged onto the street.

Clearly the two thugs were headed somewhere.

Strangely enough, they were dressed as if they were going to watch the chariot race. They wore festive clothing—clean kilts, some simple jewelry, and Snaggletooth had a red sash around his waist. Cleaned up as he was, he almost looked normal. Almost—but Zet doubted a man with a face like that would ever look normal or fit in anywhere. He was too scary looking.

The thugs were armed with nasty looking weapons. Snaggletooth had a long knife strapped to his waist. He'd polished the scabbard, so it looked somewhat decorative.

His partner had a club studded with nails. At a comment from Snaggletooth, the man laughed. He had a strip of linen in one hand, and he proceeded to wind it around the club as they walked.

Zet realized it would be concealed, but equally deadly. The nails could still harm a person—even kill them—cloth or not. A few strikes from a man that size would knock Zet down, he had no doubt of that.

But the more important issue was, where were they going? The fighters set off, their eyes looking into the distance as if seeing something they planned to do.

Should he follow, or stay and watch the workshop?

Where was the shipment?

He thought back to the way Hui had told him the answer was inside the ball.

Then his mind roamed to the bread. It seemed like a lot of work to get the roll and hollow it out, just to use as stuffing. With a frown, he glanced in the direction the twin bakers pushed the loaded cart. Snaggletooth and the thug had gone the same way.

A thought started to form, but he couldn't quite grasp it.

Then, with a cry of understanding, he leaped to his feet.

He ran.

He tore along the first few blocks. Snaggletooth and his buddy came into view. The heavily muscled fighters had nearly caught up with the bakers' cart. Zet slowed and watched.

The two thugs slowed as well, keeping pace with the bakers. They didn't quite catch up, but remained close enough to be next to the sisters in a few paces. To an outsider, it looked like they had nothing to do with one another.

But Zet knew differently.

Snaggletooth and the huge man with the concealed, barbed club were guarding that cart with their lives.

The bakers merged into the growing trickle of crowds. Zet pushed closer, joining a group of people as they exited a door. They glanced at him strangely, noting his filthy outfit. One of them fiddled in a pouch, produced a copper kite and offered it to him.

Zet shook his head. "Thank you."

The man shrugged. "Happy Opet Festival to you."

This could be a problem; Zet didn't want people noticing him, even if he knew the man was being kind. Still, he stuck near his group and watched the cart ahead. Two well-dressed ladies approached the bakers' cart. Zet could tell the ladies wanted to buy bread. The bakers, however, shook their heads no in a sharp voice.

The elegant ladies, surprised, walked on.

They were approaching an intersection. Medjay had taken up posts on either side of the roadway, and stood in full battle gear. The bakers wheeled their cart toward the road that led left.

The medjay blocked them with his long, wooden spear. "Halt!"

CHAPTER 35
PILES OF BREAD

"We need to turn here," came the sharp voice of Kakra.

"Road's closed. Go straight, please," the medjay told the twin bakers.

"The road's closed?" Kissa gasped, looking frightened.

"Festival precautions, madam."

"Where can we turn?" Kakra demanded. "We're working here. We need to make a delivery. This bread has been ordered for a special party. We need to get to the Nile!"

"The main road goes to the Nile, madam."

"Yes, but not where I need to be. I need to get farther down!"

"You'll have to carry on straight like everyone else until you get to the Avenue of the Sphinxes." He waved his fiber shield at the main road. "When you get to the waterfront, you can follow the Nile to your party."

Kakra's mouth tightened in a hard line. Kissa paled.

"Fine," Kakra said.

Then she glanced back at Snaggletooth. Under her anger, Zet read dismay mixed with fear. Snaggletooth nodded at Kakra. She wheeled the cart back into the main roadway and carried on.

They had just confirmed every one of Zet's suspicions.

The stolen jewels were hidden in the loaves of bread! The sisters must have baked them right inside so no hole in the bottom would give them away. That's how they planned to get past being searched.

No medjay would give the bread cart a second glance.

Kissa and Kakra simply had to deliver the goods to a boat. A boat, where Kemet would obviously be waiting to make his escape. The bread would be loaded. Right under everyone's noses.

Then Kemet would happily sail away with his load of stolen goods.

Clever Hui, Zet thought. In the end, the ivory ball had told Zet everything. He wondered what his best friend had had to risk getting that information. Hui must have been living in terror, between sneaking around and constructing the fake scarab and ball.

It was up to Zet now to stop that cart.

Snaggletooth glanced over his shoulder.

Zet dodged behind a noisy family. Panic gripped him, but he forced himself to calm down. Snaggletooth must not have seen him; otherwise, he'd be on him right now.

He needed to do something, but what?

Ahead of him, the kids from the family were joking around. One boy jabbed his older brother from behind with a toy sword, and then darted away.

"Quit it," the older brother said.

"What?" said the boy with sword. "Wasn't me. Must have been the evil spirit."

"Mom!"

"Stop it, both of you, that's not funny," the mother whispered in a nervous voice.

Until that moment, Zet had forgotten all about the demon army.

Zet knew the demon army didn't exist. But no one else did. He had an idea. Maybe it was time to create a demon of his own.

He followed the crowd a little further, looking for an unguarded alcove where he could slip away. He needed to get to his market square.

With the medjay blocking every side street, he needed a different route. The medjay would never let him through. He'd just have to take to the rooftops.

Fortunately, he was getting his climbing skills back. He hadn't spent this much time clambering around since Hui left home.

Music drifted from up ahead. A small band had taken up residence along the side of the street. They pounded on drums, plucked lutes, and sang about the war in Hyksos. People had stopped, and some were kicking up their heels to dance. Zet thought of his father, away fighting, and his heart swelled hearing the song.

Perfumed incense drifted thick on the morning air. He had to push now to keep the cart in sight. Men and women were approaching the bakers, trying to barter for a loaf. It was slow going. Still, he'd have to be quick.

Then he saw his chance. A dead end alley, unguarded, opened to his right. He slipped down it, blending into the dark shadows. Without pause, he ran for the farthest wall. The stones were rough, pressed into mud. His fingers and toes found handholds, and he scrambled upward. When he reached the rooftop, he bent low and sprinted over the loose tiles to the far side.

The street below was full of people, all moving toward the broader avenue he'd left behind. He glanced right and left, and saw he'd have to travel further along the roof to get a clear spot to drop back down. He climbed up another story onto a high patio full of potted plants. He had to sprint across half a dozen private terraces before he found a quiet place to climb down.

Silence met him. He recognized the lane. Usually full of people, today it was still as a Pharaoh's tomb. He ran onward. He ran until he was breathless.

He gasped in triumph when his familiar market square opened before him.

Everything was bound up tight. It was strange to see it so still.

"I hope you don't kill me for this, Geb," he said as he hurried to the herb vendor's stall. With a glance both ways, he got down on hands and knees and crawled under the tightly wrapped stall covers. It was dark, and he had to squint to see. The smells of cumin and cardamom, cinnamon and myrrh bombarded him in the confined space. It was heady and overpowering, jarring his senses to life.

CHAPTER 36
DEMON BOY

Head spinning, Zet waited for his eyes to adjust to the darkness.

The colored pyramids of herbs and spices, flours, clothing dye and crushed incense came slowly into focus. He crawled forward. A clay urn leaned up against a wood pillar. The outside was cool and damp to the touch. He pulled the cork and sniffed. Cooking oil. And, thank the gods, it was full.

He poured some slick oil out, coating himself by the handful as best he could.

"I promise, I'll repay you Geb, wherever you are," he muttered, as he reached for the flour. Then he dumped some over his head.

Next came streaks of bright blue woad, yellow cumin, and crushed red madder root. He crisscrossed his face, arms and legs with crazy, bright marks. Then it was time to go.

He only hoped he could cut off the cart on time.

After slipping out, he went to his own stall and found a length of old linen, worn paper-thin. Once folded, it made a half decent robe. Well-covered, he headed into the maze of deserted streets.

Birds dozed on the hot stones. They flew up in annoyance as he ran past.

Zet cut left and right, weaving his way closer and closer to the broad road that lead to the Avenue of the Sphinx. The sounds of the crowd grew louder. People shouting, laughing, singing.

He was nearly there.

Ahead, a medjay stood with his back to Zet, watching over the crowd.

Zet paused.

If he'd timed it right, the cart should be passing soon.

Several tense moments went by.

No cart.

What if he'd missed it? Sweat poured down his sides. Should he stay? Should he wait? Should he run ahead? His stomach clenched as his mind tore him in opposite directions.

Then, as if by a miracle, the cart wheeled into view. Kissa and Kakra were red-faced with the heat and the effort of maneuvering through the people. Snaggletooth and his henchman still tracked them, several paces behind. Under his makeshift robe, Zet started to sweat. The sackcloth tunic felt like a thousand nails scratching at him. He went to wipe his brow, but stopped himself. It would be no good ruining all that crazy paint. Instead he let it drip, stinging his eyes.

Time to go.

Just as he started forward, Kissa stumbled. Snaggletooth gave up pretending to be separate from the women. He strode forward and took up one of the cart handles. The other henchmen motioned Kakra aside, and took up the other.

Zet groaned at this unexpected development. Still, he slid past the medjay, who took no notice. There were too many other distractions to keep an eye on.

Zet shoved forward into the crowd.

People propelled him past, just to get him out from underfoot.

The cart came up quickly.

Only four people separated Zet from Snaggletooth. The thug pushed onward, deftly maneuvering the cart with its pyramid-shaped mound of bread.

With a shout, Zet threw off his robe. He leapt into the air, screaming in a high-pitched yowl. Like a demon, he tore at his hair. Eyes wild, he threw his arms around. Shouted. Howled. Screamed.

People fell back in shock.

In the heat, the oil had mixed with his sweat, and the streaks of color melted down his face, arms and legs. The scratchy burlap sack made him look even more crazed. Judging from their faces, he looked like a fiend straight from the underworld.

"The demon," a woman screamed. "It's the demon!"

"Run!" shouted another.

"We're trapped!" shouted a third.

Zet rushed this way and that, flinging his arms around, clearing a path to the cart. Only the four people guarding the bread stood their ground. Snaggletooth dove for Zet, but Zet was faster. He circled around the other side of the wheels. The henchman met him there with a swing of his deadly club.

Zet darted left. The club smashed into the cart's side. The cart shuddered under the impact. Zet skirted past the man. Kakra lunged forward, arms outstretched. Her arms closed around air as Zet jumped onto the wooden contraption. He landed on the pyramid of bread, sending loaves scattering.

"Get him," Kakra screeched, her eyes wide with fear.

Kissa fell back, her puckered scar red against her frightened face.

Snaggletooth grimaced. The huge man snatched Zet's ankle. Meaty fingers took hold of Zet's oiled skin. Zet wrenched backward, and his oily foot slid free. He scrabbled left, and saw the club coming down. More loaves scattered as he dodged the club's blow.

"Get him!" the crowd was screaming.

"Help," shouted others. "Help, medjay!"

"Come here, boy," Snaggletooth growled.

Zet scrabbled backwards to the far end of the cart, keeping his eyes on the weapons. Someone shoved him hard. Kakra. He flew forward.

As if in slow motion, he saw Snaggletooth's sword chop down. Desperate to stop himself, Zet plunged his hands deep into the mound of bread. He landed belly first, eye-to-eye with cold, hard steel. But under his fingers, he felt something strange.

Not bread. Something warm and soft and covered in fabric.

CHAPTER 37
JEWELS

Zet somersaulted backward. Snaggletooth's blade hissed past.

"There's nowhere to go, boy," Snaggletooth hissed.

"Get down from the cart," Kakra said.

The crowd had gone quiet, watching the strange spectacle.

Zet turned slowly. He could kick the bread away and reveal what lay in the bottom of the cart, if what lay there was who he thought it was. But the sides came up too high. Only the top loaves would fall away, and the bottom would still be covered. There was only one thing to do. He hoped he guessed right.

"Beware," he shouted. "This cart is cursed!" Then he grabbed a loaf and tore the bread in half.

It was empty.

Some people laughed, nervously.

The four lunged for him. He kicked and bit and got his hands around another loaf. Zet tore it open. Empty again.

The henchman landed a glancing blow against Zet's leg with his club. Nails scraped down his shin. If it had been any closer, it would have broken Zet's leg. He was starting to tire. Desperate, he got his hands on another loaf. His fingers were so greasy with sweat and oil that it flew free.

He took up a fourth one. A long, oddly shaped one.

It was heavy.

Very heavy.

He jumped down from the cart, dodging past Kakra. But Kakra caught him. She got her gnarled fingers around the loaf. Zet wouldn't let go. Their eyes met. Hers were enraged.

Zet wedged his fingers down through the crust.

He felt the bread tear.

Kakra tried to hold it together. "Stop it," she gasped.

In one swift yank, he ripped the bread in two.

From the center, a large golden collar, glittering with precious gems, fell to the paving stones. Zet dove for it. He raised it, victorious, high above his head.

"It's full of stolen jewels," he told the crowd.

"The demon turned bread into jewels!" someone shouted.

"There are jewels hidden in the bread!" shouted another.

Frenzied, people pushed forward and started pulling the loaves from the cart and tearing them open. Gold pieces were held high in triumph.

"I found one, too," shouted someone.

"Look at mine! It's a festival trick!"

Snaggletooth, his henchman, and the twins, watched in horror. They started running this way and that, trying to recover the treasure. The looting went on; people grew wild. They shouted and cheered, like it was the best party trick ever.

Then, a woman next to the cart screamed.

She clutched at her chest, looking down into the depths of it, and kept screaming.

Zet felt sick. He knew what that scream meant.

Still, he had to see, had to know for himself.

Medjay approached from all avenues, weapons raised. Trying to control the chaos.

"Put down the jewels," the nearest medjay bellowed. "All of you! I order you to put down the jewels."

Zet ignored them. He pushed his way forward. He shoved people out of the way. He didn't care about the lost jewels. He didn't care that

Snaggletooth and the others were clearing off, dispersing, leaving. Getting away.

He stumbled ahead, as if in a daze.

Then his hands were on the sturdy wooden sides of the cart. He looked down into it. Most of the bread had been removed, but a layer still covered the bottom. At the far end, the tips of two small bare feet jutted up between two loaves.

"Get away from the cart," bellowed the nearest medjay.

Zet threw himself into it anyway. He started up at the top end where it was deeper. He tossed loaves out, left and right, wild, desperate. Made a hole. His head was spinning in terror. He pulled two clear, and suddenly he was looking down into the face of his best friend.

Hui's mouth was bound with a thick, wadded strip of cloth.

But his eyes were wide open. Staring.

He was dead. It was too late. Zet thought of Hui's mother Delilah, with her curls and ready smile. His heart clenched, and he let out a muffled cry of despair. How could this be? It wasn't fair. Not Hui. Not his best friend.

"Hui," Zet said. "No."

Then, as if by a miracle, Hui's eyes blinked.

They opened slowly. Hui looked confused, groggy. He focused on Zet and registered disbelief. Then his eyes crinkled into a grin.

From behind, the medjay grabbed Zet by his burlap tunic. "I told you to . . . what's this?" he gasped, staring down at Hui.

"Help me get him out," Zet said.

It was the doorman from the night before. Together, he and Zet tossed away the last of the bread. Hui's arms and legs were bound tightly to his side. The medjay whipped out his blade and cut the bindings free.

Hui winced and lurched upright, looking left and right. "Where are they? Don't let them get away!"

"You mean these four?" a medjay said. He and several officers hauled Snaggletooth, his henchman, and the baker twins forward.

"We're innocent," Kakra cried. "I didn't know the boy was in there."

"Explain that to the courts."

"We were just following orders," she said.

"Some orders," Hui said with a laugh, leaping out of the cart to stand beside his best friend.

Snaggletooth said nothing. He knew he'd been beaten. Half of Thebes had witnessed him trying to cut Zet into pieces.

A man with a polished breastplate strode toward them. Merimose.

"Zet? Is that you under all that paint? What's going on?"

"Long story," Zet said, and quickly filled him in.

Hui rubbed his wrists. "The coast isn't clear. We still need to stop Kemet."

CHAPTER 38
KEMET

Merimose turned to Kakra. "Where were you taking this cart?"

Kakra glared at him and said nothing.

Then Kissa spoke up. "To a boat."

"Stop it," Kakra snarled at her twin sister.

"No, Kakra, I won't hold my tongue any longer." Her cheeks were flushed. "I blame myself for letting it go this far. But I won't be a part of it any longer." To Merimose, she said, "We were taking it to Kemet's boat on the Nile. It has red and gold sails, and is docked at the farthest end of the Avenue of the Sphinx."

"Show us."

"They'll have lookouts posted," Kissa said. "They'll bolt if they see medjay coming."

The officers, Zet and Hui stood there, stumped.

Zet spoke up. "I have an idea."

And so, three big medjay piled into the cart and lay on the bottom. Over them, Zet, Hui and Merimose repacked the cart with as many loaves as they could gather.

"You six," Merimose said, retrieve whatever jewels from the crowd you can. "The rest of you, fan out down the side streets and make your way to the end of the Avenue of the Sphinx. Hang back in the shadows until I give the signal."

"What about these two?" asked the medjay Zet had met the night before.

"Secure them, and take them to the station." Merimose turned to the sisters. "Kissa and Kakra, you'll push the cart to the boat. Just like you're supposed to."

Kakra glared at her twin sister. Kissa glared back.

"And don't try anything funny," Merimose said.

And so, the procession started up once again.

The Avenue of the Sphinx gleamed up ahead, its statues polished white in the hot sunshine. Meanwhile, the crowd went back to enjoying the festival. Vendors selling every type of sweetmeat lined the road, shouting and calling out to people. Thebans pushed and shoved, intent on getting to the chariot race.

Bordering the broad Avenue of the Sphinx, the Nile glimmered. Ahead, boats bobbed in the smooth band of water.

The group followed the bread cart away from the action.

A big hand clamped around Zet's forearm. Zet jumped.

"It's just me," Merimose said. "Stay back. I don't want you seen."

"I don't think they'll recognize me like this," Zet said.

"It's too dangerous."

Zet and Hui exchanged a glance. No way were they staying back. Still, Zet nodded. He and Hui let the others get ahead.

"We'll just keep low, right?" Zet said.

"Right," Hui agreed.

They crept forward, using the crowd as cover. But as the crowd thinned, that became more and more difficult.

Hui put a hand on Zet's arm. "Look, the red and gold sail."

They ducked behind a stone sphinx and watched the baker twins push the cart closer. On board the boat, a curtain flickered. No one, however, stepped out onto the deck.

"They suspect something," Zet said.

Then a boy appeared. He started to untie the ropes. They were preparing to cast off. They were going to get away!

"Why doesn't Merimose do something?" Hui said.

"How? He can't search Kemet without proof of wrongdoing. Kemet has no stolen jewels on board either. He can deny it all. He can say he didn't know what was going on."

"I'll get them out of there," Hui said. Then, in a perfect imitation of Snaggletooth, he called out, "Kemet!"

Nothing happened for a moment.

Kissa spoke up, and called, "We've brought your bread, Kemet!"

A hatch opened, and someone came on deck. It was Kemet himself. The hobbled man hurried over the boards to the rail. He looked angry.

"You're late," he called the bakers. "I thought something was wrong."

"We had some trouble," Kissa said.

"But it's all there?"

"All of it," Kissa said.

Merimose raised the whistle that hung around his neck and blew. Sharp, short and loud. Instantly, bread loaves flew everywhere. The medjay leaped out of the cart. They swarmed on board, while others swarmed out of side streets and joined them.

Kemet had given them all the proof they needed.

Kemet and his band were done.

The crooked jeweler glanced down and saw Zet and Hui on the wharf. His face darkened. He looked ready to hiss curses at them. But as Merimose bound Kemet's wrists, the jeweler's shoulders sagged. His reign as a powerful smuggler had come to a bitter end.

CHAPTER 39
ALL IS WELL

"Do you realize how great it is to be standing out here?" Hui cried. "I'm a free kid again."

Zet nodded. All would have been well, if only their mother was home safe.

And then, from the corner of his eye, he saw someone waving from an approaching boat. The boat was tiny, barely large enough to fit the three people seated in it. And it was piled high with pottery.

"Zet?" cried his mother. "Is that you?"

The relief at seeing her and Apu was so overwhelming that tears stung his eyes. At least no one could tell, between the sweat and the crazy face paint.

It was only moments before he and Hui were helping her on shore, and hearing how the potters' delivery boat had sprouted a hole, and how strange things had been going on in the village itself.

"The family who usually does the orders has left the village, and no one knows why," she said. "But I was able to find someone else to do the work. It was all very last minute. And finding the boat wasn't easy. But we need to get these orders delivered, and fast."

"I think I know just the way to do it," Zet said.

He and Hui commandeered the bakers' cart. They loaded it high with pottery.

"I could have some men deliver a set, too," Merimose said, when he'd heard the story.

"And I'll deliver these two serving bowls," Zet's mother said. "It's only two pieces, and the house isn't far from here."

By mid-morning, the deliveries were complete. All of the women were happy to finally have their special dishes. Even the angry one was impressed when she heard why the pottery hadn't come, and what lengths Zet's family had gone through to get them.

"Now want to go watch the races?" Zet said.

"Hey, I'll do anything with you dressed like a demon."

He hadn't bothered to change; there wasn't time. "I thought the women would be scared, but they all loved it," Zet said.

"Go figure," Hui said, grinning. "Next thing you know, they'll be hosting demon dress up parties." They'd reached the edge of the chariot races. "Look, I think the Royal Mother likes it, too," he said, pointing to a golden pavilion whose curtains fluttered in the faint breeze.

In it, the Royal Mother was indeed staring at Zet. So was Pharaoh himself.

The ground shook, as a chariot roared past.

Then came a second, and third.

Wheels glinted in the light, and the riders looked glorious in their uniforms.

Hui wore a huge grin. "This is like old times. Except better. We just had an adventure for real."

"You're not kidding, talk about adventure. I thought you were dead," Zet said.

"It's not that easy to kill me. And speaking of which, now that I'm out of work, maybe I can help you with your side business."

"Side business? What side business."

"You know, the whole Secret Agent Zet thing."

"Secret Agent Zet, huh?"

"It has a catchy ring, doesn't it?"

"Uh, not really," Zet said, laughing. "I'm not exactly a secret agent."

Hui ignored him. "And everyone knows a secret agent needs a side-kick." He waggled his eyebrows and elbowed Zet. "How about it? You and me? Solving crimes in the city?"

Zet groaned and rolled his eyes.

But Hui's attention was elsewhere. He grabbed Zet's arm and pointed. "Over there. A girl calling for help. Quick, we need to save her!"

In a panic, Zet turned to look.

It was Kat. But she wasn't in trouble. She was waving her arms at them, laughing and screaming and jumping up and down.

Zet groaned. He couldn't believe he fell for it.

"I'm throwing you in the river," Zet said.

"You'll have to catch me first," Hui replied.

Together, they took off into the bright, Theban afternoon.

HISTORICAL NOTE FROM THE AUTHOR

This story is a work of fiction. While none of the characters mentioned actually existed, the setting is very much as it would have been during the time when this book was set.

The Egyptians kept very good notes. They loved to write things down. Using their records we can imagine what life was like—from their clothing to the marketplaces, from their foods to their customs. Most families kept a household shrine. Bes was a popular household god as he was considered a protector of families, particularly mothers and children.

Workshops, such as the Kemet workshop, were a popular way to teach skills to the next generation of craftsmen. Rather than attend school, a workshop provided pupils with an education in a specific craft. The jewelry created during this era is still marveled at today.

For more amazing ancient Egypt facts, along with games and activities, be sure and visit my blog: www.egyptabout.com

ACKNOWLEDGMENTS

To all the amazing people who helped pull this story together, thank you. Special thanks to Scott Lisetor, Peter, Judy, Jill and Sarah Wyshynski, Sharon Brown, Amanda Budde-Sung, Ellie Crowe, Adria Estribou, Glenn Desy and David Desy.

CONTINUE THE ADVENTURE

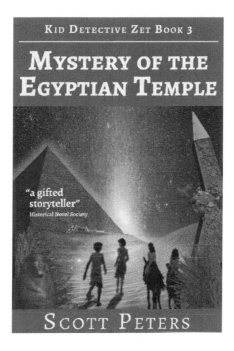

Continue the adventure with history's favorite young detectives!

coming soon:

Mystery of the Egyptian Mummy (Kid Detective Zet #4)

Manufactured by Amazon.ca
Bolton, ON

13393445R00085